"I care abou [...]
God's sake, I' [...]
you."

She felt her mouth d [...]

Had he really said he [...] ing in love with her? Tentative hope flared.

"Really?"

"Yes, but you need to understand—I can't change who I am. I'm falling for you, but I still don't want a family."

Her brief feeling of euphoria faded. "You can't mean that."

"I do. You're the one who told me adults make choices. What if this is the choice I've made?" When she opened her mouth to interrupt him, he raised a hand. "Some people aren't the family type. They can't cope with it. My parents were a prime example. If you can live with that part of me, then you're welcome to come in."

She stared at him, unable to believe he'd tossed her an ultimatum. He loved her and she loved him, but she couldn't accept what he was saying. No matter how badly she wanted him, she couldn't make herself step over the threshold.

"You have no idea how much I wish I could change for you. But I can't."

Slowly, quietly, giving her every chance to stop him, he closed the door.

Laura Iding loved reading as a child, and when she ran out of books she readily made up her own, completing a little detective mini-series when she was twelve. But, despite her aspirations for being an author, her parents insisted she look into a 'real' career, so the summer after she turned thirteen she volunteered as a Candy Striper and fell in love with nursing. Now, after twenty years of experience in trauma/critical care, she's thrilled to combine her career and her hobby into one—writing Medical Romance™ for Harlequin Mills & Boon®. Laura lives in the northern part of the United States and spends all her spare time with her two teenage kids (help!), a daughter and a son, and her husband. Enjoy!

Recent titles by the same author:

THE FLIGHT DOCTOR'S RESCUE
THE FLIGHT DOCTOR'S LIFELINE
THE FLIGHT DOCTOR'S EMERGENCY

CHAPTER ONE

HEAVY, humid air intermingled with the fragrant scent of tropical flowers surrounded Dr Moriah Howe as she stepped outside the hotel. The soothing sound of ocean waves crashing on the beach made her smile.

Peru. It was great to be back in a country well known for its eternal sunshine and friendly people. A whole year had passed since her last mission here, and she was more than ready to get started.

They would meet with prospective patients in the clinic first. Moriah walked along the unique circular street, heading from the hotel that housed the Litmann and Granger plastic surgery team to Trujillo hospital. A large stone sculpture stood in the center of the city and she paused for a moment to flip a coin into the well around it.

The only wish she had was to keep memories of Dr Blake Powers buried deep in the past, where they belonged. She planned to use this impromptu trip to purge any lingering caring-too-much-for-him thoughts from her heart, once and for all.

She'd almost reached the hospital when an older

Peruvian woman with gray hair and wearing a bright red dress rushed toward her, grabbed her arm and began speaking in very rapid Spanish.

Moriah frowned and searched her rusty memory for the proper words. "What? I'm sorry, tell me again what is wrong?"

"My daughter. She needs a doctor. Come with me." The gray-haired woman tugged on her arm and Moriah willingly followed. Thankfully, they weren't far from the hospital, so additional medical help would be easy to summon.

The older woman showed her to a car with a passenger in the front seat. Moriah blanched. It was obvious the poor woman was in the throes of intense labor.

"Breathe through the pain, that's it." Trying to remain calm, Moriah placed her hand on the woman's taut belly, feeling the strength of the contraction. As an anesthesiologist, she'd completed her required stint in obstetrics, but primarily to gain expertise in placing epidural catheters and preparing for crash C-sections, not actually delivering babies.

"All right, we need to get you into the emergency department." A deep sense of urgency caused Moriah to glance around, seeking more help, but the hour was still early, and there weren't any other people on the street yet. She wasn't sure why the woman had stopped the car here, but maybe they could get a wheelchair from the hospital. She touched the older woman lightly on the arm.

"You need to go to the emergency department, ask for a wheelchair and bring it back here."

The woman nodded in understanding and hurried

off, moving surprisingly fast. Moriah knelt beside the open passenger door and spoke to the pregnant woman in a calm voice. "Hello, my name is Moriah and I'm one of the American doctors visiting here for a few weeks. Your baby is anxious to be born, so as soon as your mother gets back we'll wheel you into the hospital."

"My name is Rasha." The pregnant woman spoke between panting breaths. "There is a lot of pain and pressure. I need to push."

"No, don't push yet." Moriah banked a flare of panic. She didn't want this baby born here in the car, when they were so close to the hospital.

Rasha moaned in pain and Moriah rubbed a soothing hand over the woman's belly. She had always longed to have a big family like her own one day, but watching the grimace playing across Rasha's pretty features reminded her that the process of giving birth wasn't easy. "You're doing fine, just hang in there a little longer. I'll breathe with you during the next contraction, all right?"

Rasha nodded and together they made it through the next contraction. By Moriah's estimate, the contractions were close, only two minutes apart. Using the stethoscope around her neck, she listened to the baby's heartbeat, glad to hear it beating strong and fast. She was about to start laying on the horn to get attention when Rasha's mother returned, hurrying over with a wheelchair and a Peruvian ED nurse.

"I haven't been able to examine her progress, but I did hear good fetal heart tones and her contractions are two minutes apart." Moriah helped Rasha out of the car, into the wheelchair.

"Thanks. Let's get her inside." The Peruvian nurse pushed Rasha across the street and to the ED doors. Moriah followed, intent on staying long enough to make sure Rasha was settled in before heading over to the clinic where her patients waited.

The ED doctor shouted orders and rapid bursts of Spanish flew amongst the health-care team. Moriah's eyes widened, impressed by their effortless efficiency as they took charge of the situation, getting Rasha into a room and examining her. Rasha held firmly onto her hand so Moriah made one of the entourage in the room.

"I need to examine her." The ED doctor raised a brow at Moriah questioningly.

She understood what he silently asked. "Rasha, do you want me to leave?" she said in a low voice.

"No." Rasha shook her head, hanging on even tighter to Moriah's hand. "Please, stay. I wish Manuel was here, too."

Moriah didn't get a chance to question her about Manuel, whom she assumed was the baby's father, because the ED doctor spoke up.

"The baby is crowning, she's ready to deliver. Call the OB doctor now." He began to prepare for the delivery as the nurse hurried from the room to make the call.

Thank heavens they'd gotten her inside when they had. Moriah wondered where Rasha's mother was, but there wasn't a spare hand to be had and she couldn't bring herself to leave Rasha alone to find the older woman.

The OB doctor arrived. He agreed with the ED doctor's assessment. "There isn't time to move her upstairs. We'll deliver the baby here."

"All right, Rasha, soon you will be able to push." Moriah stroked the young woman's hair reassuringly. "Just a little more patience and you'll hold your baby in your arms."

The OB doctor prepped the area, then glanced up at Rasha. "With the next contraction, push."

Finally. Moriah was almost as relieved as Rasha that the time had come to push. A few contractions later, the baby was born.

Sheer awe intertwined with bitter-sweet longing as Moriah gazed at the tiny miracle in Rasha's arms. "A girl. Rasha, you have a beautiful baby girl." Moriah laughed as the baby cried. Rasha laughed and cried, too.

"She is a good weight, 3.2 kilograms. Congratulations." The OB doctor finished caring for the baby then wrapped her in a blanket and gave her to Rasha.

"*Gracias*. Thank you so much."

"You're welcome," the OB doctor responded, smiling.

Moriah grinned. "Let me find your mother. I'm sure she'd like to see her granddaughter."

"Yes." Rasha nodded, gazing adoringly at her baby girl.

Moriah found Rasha's mother in the waiting room and quickly ushered the woman inside, where she immediately began to croon over the baby. Satisfied the family was together and doing fine, Moriah made her excuse to go.

"I'm expected at the clinic, but congratulations

again on your beautiful baby. I'll come back later," she promised.

"Thanks for all your help," Rasha's mother said, not for the first time.

Moriah nodded, then slipped out of the room. She longed to have a family of her own, and had briefly, foolishly, harbored thoughts that it would be with Blake, but her dream wasn't meant to be.

She wasn't going to dwell on the past now and ruin her good mood. She stepped outside, where the hot, humid air seemed even more intense. February in Peru was the exact opposite weather from what her family was experiencing at home, in the midwestern part of the States. She made a mental note to let her siblings know she had arrived safely.

The clinic, adjacent to the hospital, was where the patients would be seen and screened prior to having surgery.

Moriah made her way through the crowd, in an effort to find the specific clinic assigned for her to use.

Patients were just starting to line up, so her brief foray into obstetrics hadn't put her too far behind. There was a table with refreshments for staff and patients, and she helped herself to a glass of tangy papaya juice.

Someone jostled her from behind. She lifted her arm to avoid spilling juice on her lab coat.

"Sorry about that."

The deep, achingly familiar masculine voice had Moriah turning sharply, then staring in shock as she recognized the tall, blond-haired surgeon. She nearly choked on a mouthful of papaya juice in her haste to swallow. Her voice squeaked. "Blake."

His blue eyes flared in recognition. "Moriah."

For a long moment, she stared at him in shock. Blake? Here in Peru? How could that be? Six feet tall, he towered over her, wearing a lab coat over his casual slacks and shirt, looking far more handsome than he had a right to be.

"What are you doing here?" she asked, her sharp tone belying her leaping pulse.

"Didn't you hear? I was asked to come on this trip to replace Ed Granger. His wife, Diane, has been diagnosed with breast cancer." He paused, then added in a slightly defensive tone, "I couldn't say no. He lives for this mission. I couldn't let him down."

"Of course I heard about Diane." Fate certainly had a sick sense of humor, Moriah thought sourly. "I'm here as her replacement."

So much for her plan of getting Blake out of her system. Why hadn't she thought to ask which surgeon had agreed to cover Ed? The group hadn't traveled to Peru on the same flight—half of them had arrived a day earlier. Her hand tightened on her juice. "I couldn't say no either. For one thing, all of my immunizations are up to date from last year. For another, Diane lives for this mission as much as Ed does."

"I know." Blake nodded, his gaze unreadable. "So. Here we are, together again, in beautiful Peru."

She stifled the urge to toss her juice in his face. Forcing herself to remain calm, she lifted her chin. "Don't flatter yourself, Blake. We're not here *together*. I'm sure we can manage to stay out of each other's way."

"Of course we can." Blake cleared his throat then met her gaze with a concerned look. "I'm sorry about Diane. I know how close the two of you are."

"Thanks. Diane is strong, she'll pull through this." Moriah stoutly refused to believe otherwise.

"I'm sure she will, especially with your help and support." Blake's tone was soft, comforting.

Just like he'd been last year, holding her so sweetly after they'd heard the news of Ryan's death. Dammit, she didn't want to remember how wonderful Blake had been. She didn't want to like him. And she especially didn't want to remember how it had felt to make love with him.

To have sex with him, she bluntly amended. A one-night stand wasn't anything more than casual sex. A cold hard fact she needed to remember.

"Let's get started." Moriah gulped her drink, set the empty juice glass down, and glanced around. "I'll take this clinic here."

"Fine. I'll be down the hall."

He probably figured taking the clinic farthest away from her was being helpful. It wasn't. Not when his presence here, thousands of miles from home, was a living, breathing reminder of a painful past.

Blake was totally the wrong man for her, just as Ryan had been. Why on earth couldn't she convince her heart she was better off without him?

Moriah sank into a chair in the cluttered clinic, feeling strangely exhilarated, despite her weary eyes and sore back. The constant stream of patients had taken her mind off her own problems, helping to put things in perspective.

These people were so happy to be considered for surgery. Planning ways to help them, especially the children, made her remember all the reasons she'd been thrilled to return. Granted, the Litmann and Granger plastic surgery group could only stay for three weeks, but there was so much they could accomplish, even in that short a time frame.

They could help fix the burns, the injuries, the birth defects.

Moriah opened her eyes when Blake and George Litmann entered the room. Deep in discussion, they didn't appear to notice her sitting there.

"We've made a great start. There is a list of twenty patients with high-priority injuries," Blake was saying. "The youngest is barely three months old, the oldest a man in his forties. We're going to be very busy."

"Maybe we need to focus our efforts on the children," George said thoughtfully. "Not that the older adults shouldn't get a chance at surgery, but the youngest certainly have the most to lose."

"But did you see him? There is so much scar tissue from his burns on his face and chest. We can't say no when he needs our help," Blake argued, threading his fingers through his hair in an aggrieved motion.

George sighed. "I know. We'll try to find room for him on the schedule."

"If we operate on Sunday, we can squeeze him in." Blake's troubled tone betrayed his concern, and Moriah felt her hard countenance softening. She simply couldn't seem to stay mad at him.

"I'll do his anesthesia on Sunday, if it helps." She

spoke up, alerting them to her presence. She was a medical professional. Surely she could deal with Blake if she focused on work and nothing more. "I agree with Blake. We should try to do as many cases as possible."

"There are only so many hours in a day," George reminded her. "And only so many operating suites."

She knew he was right, but she was determined each patient's needs would be met. "Are we finished for today?"

"Yeah, although we'll have another long day tomorrow." Blake kept his tone polite, yet distant.

Moriah nodded. "All right, so we have three rooms and five surgeons, with five accompanying anesthesiologists teamed together to rotate through the rooms. Depending on how many hours each case actually needs, we may have some wiggle room in the schedule."

"Yeah, plus we're doing more training with the Peruvian surgeons from last year. They're anxious to do some of the cases, too," Blake pointed out.

Without warning, a small, dark-haired boy darted through the doorway. His brown eyes widened in surprise and he skidded to a halt when he noticed the three of them standing there.

"*La médica?*" His gaze zoomed in on Moriah.

His face was familiar and with a puzzled frown she tried to place him. "Henri? Is that you?"

"Dr Moriah!" His dark face broke into a hopeful grin. "You remember."

"Of course I remember. You were one of my favorite patients." She glanced over his shoulder to the empty hallway with a frown. "Where's your mother? Didn't she come with you?"

The boy's smile dimmed as he shook his head.

"How are you?" She couldn't tell how well his leg had healed. Last year, Blake had released a bad contracture on his severely burned right foot. She slanted him a glance, wondering if he remembered Henri, too, but his oblique gaze didn't tell her anything.

Then Blake stepped forward. "How about showing us your leg?"

Henri obligingly lifted one leg of his pants and flexed his foot. Blake nodded as if pleased, and Moriah understood. The boy didn't have full range of motion, but he was clearly much better off than the last time they'd seen him. In his mad dash across the room, she hadn't noticed a limp.

"Your leg looks great." She smiled at the boy. "But why did you come back to see us?"

His brown eyes were earnest as he glanced between her and Blake. "Remember? You told me you would fix my fingers when you came back." He held up his hand to display the three mangled fingers of his left hand where burns had contracted the digits beyond recognition, making them useless. "See?"

"That's right, I do remember. We didn't have time to complete your surgery last time." Moriah met Blake's gaze. "There's a place for Henri on the schedule, right?"

Blake took the boy's damaged hand in his and gently examined it. "He's lucky he has some use of his index finger and thumb," he said doubtfully. "He'll gain some additional movement from repairing the three injured digits, but not anything close to normal function."

"Please? *Por favor?*" Henri's brown eyes were big enough to overpower his whole face.

"Blake, we did promise him, last year," Moriah reminded him. Blake might be hell on women, but he was a compassionate doctor. His determination to put his patients' needs first was one of the traits she most admired in him. "Gaining any movement in his hand is worth the effort. I'll stay late, or come in early. This surgery won't take long."

Blake glanced at George who shrugged helplessly. Then he smiled. "Sure, why not? We'll squeeze him in."

"*Gracias!*" Henri beamed at Moriah again. "See you later."

"Bye, Henri." She reached out and smoothed a hand over his tousled black hair. She was somewhat surprised Henri remembered her so well, to the point he'd sought her out again a year later.

The boy slipped from the room far more quietly than he'd entered. He was a great kid. In fact, Henri reminded her of Mitch, her oldest nephew. They were about the same age, and both seemed always to run from point A to point B, constantly in a hurry to get somewhere. Last year they'd had trouble keeping Henri off his injured leg long enough for it to heal.

Longing for a family of her own pierced her heart.

Her relationship with Ryan, her former fiancé, had disintegrated when he'd broken off their engagement months before he'd died, because he hadn't been able to give up his player lifestyle.

Then she'd fallen hard for Blake, Ryan's best friend and bachelor buddy, who had comforted her the night they'd learned of Ryan's death, then had left her the next day to move on to another woman. His rejection had sliced deep, although she shouldn't have been so naive as to think she could change him.

She sighed. She really had a lousy track record with men.

CHAPTER TWO

BLAKE'S gut twisted with regret as his gaze drifted once again toward Moriah. Damn, she was more beautiful than he'd remembered. He was disturbed by his physical reaction to her. The way his fingers itched to slide into the wealth of dark hair she'd pulled back into a clip at her nape to loosen the strands so they draped around her shoulders. The way her luminous brown eyes and softly curved mouth promised infinite pleasure. She wasn't the right woman for him, but his body hadn't seemed to care about that, the way it had reacted to her instantly when he'd bumped into her earlier that morning.

He'd come on this mission as a favor to Ed Granger. Never once in his wildest imagination had he expected Moriah would be here, too. Hell, on the interminable flight out, he'd passed the time flirting with some nurse whose name now escaped him. But seeing Moriah here, he knew with fatalistic certainty he was going to make the same mistake as before.

He didn't understand why he was still so very attracted to her, but he was. He wanted her with a depth that scared the living heck out of him.

He'd known her for years, since he'd been best friends with her fiancé, Ryan. After her relationship with Ryan had disintegrated, the tiny devil on his shoulder had constantly nudged him, reminding him she was free. Here in Peru last year, they'd grown closer, finally making love on their last night together. But the next morning he'd panicked, knowing that with her love of family she'd expect more than he was willing to give.

So he'd ended up hurting her, just like Ryan had.

Realistically, he'd figured it was better to break their budding relationship off early, before things had grown too complicated. They wanted different things from their futures. She was a woman who wanted to settle down, to have a family, while he simply didn't. Kids were a huge responsibility, one he didn't want to tackle.

He and Moriah were at completely opposite ends of the spectrum on this crucial matter, and always would be. So he had to be strong. To avoid hurting her again, he somehow needed to find a way to keep distance between them.

George Litmann's presence wasn't enough of a deterrent, though. No, he needed more than that to keep himself from hauling her into his arms and kissing her senseless. He needed to be further away, like rocket-blasted to another planet. Dammit. Where in the hell was the blonde, Claire what's-her-name, when he needed her?

"It's late. Should we head back to the hotel for dinner?" George asked.

"Hmm." Blake couldn't tear his eyes off Moriah. She seemed lost in her thoughts, gazing through the empty doorway where the boy, Henri, had disappeared. Her eyes were filled with such heartfelt longing, reminding him only too clearly of the dark pain he'd seen in her eyes last year.

"Moriah? Would you join us?" George asked.

"Huh?" With a guilty start, she brought her eyes to his, then just as quickly glanced away. "Oh, no, thanks anyway. I have a patient I need to see."

"A patient?" Blake frowned. "You mean from the group we saw today?"

"No, not from the clinic. This morning I helped a pregnant woman avoid giving birth in her car." Moriah's face broke into a beaming smile, sucker-punching him in the gut. "I stayed with her while she delivered a beautiful baby girl. I'm heading over to check on her."

He wasn't surprised she wanted to go back and see the baby. Did he need another reminder of how wrong they were for each other? When George glanced at him questioningly, he shook his head. "Go ahead, I have a few things I need to do yet." He'd actually promised to have dinner with the blonde from the plane. He should have been more than ready to move on.

But he couldn't seem to drum up enthusiasm for his date.

George nodded, then left the clinic, walking out with Moriah. It took all Blake's willpower and then some not to follow them.

He sat heavily in a chair and cradled his head in his hands. Self-loathing dripped and burned like battery acid down the length of his esophagus.

He'd hurt Moriah once—he had no business resurrecting the past all over again. She'd taken the news of Ryan's death hard, even though they had no longer been engaged by the time he'd died. She didn't need him crawling back to her, after the way he'd left her before.

Blake scrubbed his face with his hands, as if he could erase the image of Moriah's hurt expression that was permanently etched in his brain. Then, with a determined effort, he stood and headed to the hotel lobby where Claire what's-her-name was waiting for him.

Except he'd lost all interest in pursuing a romantic interlude with her, or anyone else. Still, he forced a welcoming smile on his face, determined to enjoy some harmless flirtation with a woman who knew the score. It wouldn't be the first time he'd whiled away the hours with one woman while knowing his heart belonged to another.

Hell. He was a pro at keeping up the pretense by now.

Hours later, Blake took a walk outside in a vain effort to clear the scent of Claire's cloying, flowery perfume from his head. Man, the woman just hadn't stopped talking, idle chit-chat he'd barely been able to concentrate on, until the end of the meal had finally approached and she'd gotten bolder, telling him straight out he was welcome to come to her room after dinner, if he so desired.

He didn't, so he'd claimed he needed to meet with one of the Peruvian doctors at the hospital about arranging the logistics of the operating room schedule, and had made a quick escape.

Taking a slow, deep, cleansing breath, he forced himself to face the truth. These next three weeks were going to be the longest in his entire life. No way would he be able to convince himself he was attracted to another woman when Moriah was close enough to see. To smell. To touch.

Sounds of footsteps on the road ahead of him made him squint through the darkness to see who else had sought the quietness of the night. When he rounded a bend in the curved road, he caught sight of a dark-haired woman. His jaw tightened in recognition and he bit back a groan.

Moriah.

Of course, the one woman in the whole world who was off-limits to him would be the one within reach. He should turn and head in the opposite direction before she saw him and they were forced to exchange polite greetings while he vainly tried to ignore the sizzling electric awareness that leapt between them whenever they were within two feet of each other.

An awareness he knew wasn't completely one-sided.

Too late. His traitorous legs carried him forward just as she turned to see who he was. Her eyes widened with recognition.

"Hello, Blake."

"Moriah."

An awkward silence hovered. Would it always be like this between them? He longed for the early days of friendship, before he'd let his desire overrule logic. Yet even now the unruly desire was difficult to control.

His hungry gaze feasted upon her. She was breathtaking in the moonlight. She hadn't changed much in the past year, and a quick glance at her hand showed she hadn't gotten married during the months they'd spent apart.

He had no right to feel delighted about the absence of a ring. She deserved to find a man who would eagerly give her the family she desired. She deserved to find peace in a life he had no interest in pursuing.

The fresh citrus scent clinging to her teased his nostrils. Memories tumbled through his head. A night like this one, when a comforting embrace had changed into something very different. His body stirred at the memory. Her soft frame pressed urgently against his chest, her mouth hot and demanding beneath his...

Inside the pockets of his lab coat, his hands clenched into fists. Why did he respond to her like this? Especially when he hadn't seen her in months? What deviant gene in his DNA longed for a woman who didn't want the same things as he did from life?

Damn. He needed to find a way to stay away from her. And soon.

"Well, it was nice chatting with you, Blake." She broke the tangible silence between them with a tiny bit of sarcasm. "But it's been a long day. Good night."

"We need to talk." The words popped out of his mouth before he could stop them.

She paused in the act of leaving, and partially turned toward him. In the dim light shining from the hotel windows, he could see her dark gaze was wary. "Really? About what?"

Tell her, the tiny voice in his head urged. *Tell her the truth. After all this time, she deserves to know why you hurt her by walking away. By finding someone else*.

"The surgery schedule." *Coward*, he mentally berated himself. "We start tomorrow with only three rooms. I think things will be easier for both of us if you work with one of the other surgeons."

"Fine with me." The way she'd readily agreed with his suggestion set his teeth on edge. "Take care, Blake."

"Good night." He called himself several kinds of a fool as he watched her head back into the hotel. Instinctively, he began to follow her inside, then realized what he was doing and abruptly turned away.

What was he thinking?

Blake resisted the urge to bang his head against the bright yellow stucco-covered building. Stupid. He was so damn stupid. Moriah had happily-ever-after written all over her. Hell, hadn't she spent hours telling him her dream of having a large family with Ryan? She'd come from a large family herself, the third youngest of eight, and longed for the same closeness for her children.

While he was a man who needed his solitude, his space. He didn't have anything personal against kids— they were fine for people who wanted to have them. But his limited experience with children had been enough to cement his decision not to have any.

He liked his privacy. He liked peace and quiet, especially in the mornings, when the sun was just peeking over the horizon. He liked dedicating his life to his career, not feeling torn between the demands of his work and the even more emotional demands of a family. He didn't regret the choices he'd made.

So why did his body seem focused solely on Moriah, the one woman whose feelings were the complete opposite of his?

Blake pressed his eyes against the magnifying goggles he was using to repair a three-year-old patient's severe facial burn. He'd already debrided the affected area and was trying to place a full-thickness skin graft over the worst of the damaged tissue. This was the most delicate part of the surgery, but as he operated he was keenly aware of Moriah seated mere inches from him, monitoring little Anita's anesthesia. Despite his attempts to arrange otherwise, Moriah had been the anesthesiologist assigned to his first case. Rather than create a scene in front of George that would have required some sort of explanation, he'd left the room assignments as they had been and tried to ignore her presence while he concentrated on the delicate surgery.

He was failing miserably on the ignoring part.

For years, he'd admired Moriah from afar. Her laughter. The way she smiled, so her whole face lit up like a Christmas tree. Her patience and skill as an anesthesiologist. The way she'd go from prim and proper to wild woman with one deep kiss.

"I'm having trouble here."

Her voice drew him from his musings. He lifted his head from his microscope and met her gaze. "What is it?"

"Anita's pulse ox is dropping." All he could see of Moriah was her deep brown eyes above her surgical mask, but they were filled with worry. "I can also hear wheezes through both sides of her lungs. I think she might have asthma."

"Was asthma reflected in the pre-op assessment?" Blake asked, turning his attention to the task at hand. The sutures he'd placed on the facial skin graft were nearly complete, the worst part of the surgery almost over. He needed little Anita to hang on a little longer.

"No, her mother denied she had asthma." Moriah's tone was filled with doubt. "I suspected she might, because her lungs sounded a little tight even then, but I didn't push."

"Don't beat yourself up about it. We'd have probably taken the risk anyway. Her burns were pretty severe." Blake placed the final suture, then raised his head in relief. "The graft is finished. All I need to do is dress the donor graft site and she'll be ready to roll."

"I'm giving her a dose of solu-medrol," Moriah told him. "Let's hope this works."

"Good. Keep me posted on how she's doing."

"I will," Moriah said. He didn't doubt her for a minute. She was one of the best anesthesiologists he'd ever worked with. Maybe that was partly the reason he hadn't pushed George into changing room assignments.

A few minutes later, she announced, "Pulse 130, BP 96 over 40, pulse ox still marginal at 90 per cent. If her pulse ox drops any lower, we may have to abort the case."

Aborting the surgery wasn't optimal, but he understood Moriah's concern. Prepared for the worst, he concentrated on placing one tiny suture at a time. These burns were the most difficult procedures they'd perform over the next few weeks. The contracture releases were less complicated and there were a few cleft lip and cleft palate repairs to be done as well. All types of surgery posed a risk, especially when there were so many potential complications, and the risk was even higher when your patient was barely three years old.

"Anita's pulse ox is still dropping, Blake, it's hovering at 89 per cent. Do you think I should give her another dose of steroids?" Moriah's voice wavered with uncharacteristic uncertainty.

"Yes. I'm almost finished here." He wished he had time to reassure Moriah, but he'd just have to talk to her later. He glanced at the nurse who hovered nearby. "Will you help me dress this graft site? We need to get this patient finished quickly, before her condition deteriorates further."

"Of course, Doctor." The scrub nurse began dressing the wound, a job he normally preferred to do himself. Still, he knew she was more than competent at the task.

He placed the last suture, then carefully examined his work. Not because he thought it was the best he'd ever seen, but to make sure he hadn't missed anything.

"I'm all finished here. Go ahead and reverse her," he told Moriah.

"Are they ready for us in PACU?" she asked.

All patients went to the post-anesthesia recovery

unit after surgery. The nurses there were skilled in bringing patients out of anesthesia and getting their pain under control before they went to their rooms.

"They're ready."

"Good. I'm going to extubate her, I think breathing against the vent is making her worse." Moriah removed the tiny pediatric-sized endotracheal tube, then covered Anita's face with an oxygen mask. Blake noticed she kept a wary eye on Anita's face as he helped her move the patient over to a gurney and wheel her into the PACU, located down the hall and round the corner from the OR suites.

Greta, another American nurse, stepped forward to help settle Anita. They didn't have all the equipment normally found in the States, but in some ways he liked that part. It forced them to examine the patient more closely, rather than depend on machines, which were known to malfunction at times. Greta listened to the girl's heart and lungs the old-fashioned way, with a stethoscope.

Without warning, the three-year-old's face turned a dusky shade of blue. Greta grabbed an ambu-bag with an oxygen mask attached, placing it securely over the child's face.

"Dr Howe! She's having a laryngospasm. She can't breathe!"

CHAPTER THREE

"BE CAREFUL, try to avoid the sutures I just put in. If the skin flap goes bad, I'll need to do the entire operation over again."

Moriah peered into Anita's throat with the laryngoscope, trying to visualize the tracheal opening through the swollen tissue. She had no intention of ruining Blake's handiwork—Anita wouldn't tolerate further surgery. But the newly placed split-thickness skin graft on Anita's face was the least of her concerns just now. Maintaining an airway was one of the more important parts of an anesthesiologist's job. If she didn't get this endotracheal tube into the child soon, she'd die.

"Come on," she muttered under her breath as she tried to slide the tube into Anita's tiny throat. The spasms were so bad, the tube wouldn't go in.

Moriah tossed the useless endotracheal tube aside and grabbed the face mask and ambu-bag to give the girl some oxygen. She tried to hyperventilate her. The dusky color faded but not by much.

"Do you want me to try?" Blake offered.

"No." Moriah shook her head. Blake would certainly know how to intubate a patient but, as a surgeon, it wasn't his area of expertise. "There isn't time. I need to trach her." Moriah strove to remain calm, although she had never done a tracheostomy on a child this young. "Find me a scalpel, splinter forceps and a size-three trach."

"Here." Greta quickly handed her the requested supplies.

"Get her strapped onto the gurney so she doesn't move," Moriah instructed as she prepped the child's throat with antimicrobial solution.

Greta did as she'd been asked while Blake stepped off to the side, giving them plenty of room to work. She appreciated his sensitivity. As a surgeon, it couldn't be easy for him to relinquish control. Taking a deep, calming breath, Moriah used the scalpel to make a small incision in the child's throat. With tiny forceps, she opened the tissue enough to thread the tracheostomy tube into the opening in Anita's airway.

"Greta, can you help me secure this?" Holding the trach in place with one hand, Moriah quickly connected the ambu-bag directly to the tracheostomy tube so she could give the child several deep breaths. Anita's color instantly returned to normal and Moriah breathed a sigh of relief.

"She's fine now." Greta's voice held admiration as she tied the tracheostomy tube in place. "Thank heavens. I was worried there for a moment."

"Me, too," Moriah admitted. "That was too close for comfort. We could have lost her." Doubt gnawed at her. Had she made the wrong choice in extubating Anita so soon after surgery?

"You did the right thing, Moriah." Blake's gentle tone caused her to glance across at him in surprise. He must have read the uncertainty on her face. "You were having trouble oxygenating her during the case with the endotracheal tube in place. You didn't know about her asthma. Any patient can have a laryngospasm, it's a common risk of anesthesia."

"I know." His blue eyes were calm, steady. Logically, her brain knew Blake was right: any patient could have a laryngospasm. But the memory of Anita's dusky blue face was difficult to forget. A few minutes longer and the results could have been catastrophic.

Shaking off her self-doubt, she squared her shoulders. There wasn't time to dwell on her decision, not when there were other patients waiting for surgery. "All right, Greta, we're going to start the next case. Keep a close eye on this little girl for me."

"I will," Greta promised. The PACU nurse reached into her bag of stuffed toys and chose a floppy-eared dog for Anita, placing the animal on the bed for the girl to see when she woke up.

Moriah smiled at Anita's peaceful face. The last time they'd been here, the animals had been a huge hit with the children. The kids held their stuffed toys as if they were gold, smiling in spite of what must have been agonizing post-operative pain. Sometimes the silliest gifts were appreciated the most.

"Wait a minute." Blake caught her arm as she tried to walk past him to return to the OR suites. His brows were pulled together in a concerned frown. "Are you sure you're all right? Maybe you should take a break before we start the next case."

"No, I don't want to fall behind schedule." Moriah was hyperaware of the sizzling electric shock that tingled along her nerves at Blake's warm hand on her arm. His touch made the heavy blanket of exhaustion cloaking her shoulders dissipate. How did he manage to make her feel special with a single touch, when other men left her cold?

Irritated with herself, she pulled away and tried to concentrate on what needed to be done. "I can't bear the thought of not getting to all the patients on the list."

"We won't fall behind." Blake steered her toward the physicians' lounge. "Five minutes with your feet up will do wonders."

Actually, Moriah knew his feet probably ached more than hers did. He had to stand to do surgery, while she could sit. Giving in, she headed for the lounge.

"Ah-h." Blake smiled in pure ecstasy as he propped his feet on the table. "Feels wonderful."

"I bet." She couldn't begrudge him a few minutes of rest, even if being here like this with him was akin to torture. She was supposed to be purging him from her system, not longing for something she couldn't have.

"Tell me, how is your postpartum mom doing?"

She was surprised he'd remembered, although she shouldn't have been. Blake had a great memory for detail—it was one of the things made him such a good surgeon. She shrugged. "I'm not sure. I went to visit her last night, but the nurses wouldn't let me in while she was trying to breast-feed. I plan to go back later today."

"Sounds like she's doing fine, then."

"Maybe I'll go take another peek at Anita." Moriah needed to reassure herself the girl was all right.

"Greta would come and find you if something was wrong," Blake pointed out.

"I know." The real truth was, sitting here and chatting with him was nowhere near relaxing. Being on a different continent might have helped. "I'll meet you in the operating room in a few minutes."

"All right. Moriah?" he said before she could leave.

She paused in the doorway. "Yes?"

"It's great working with you again."

It was on the tip of her tongue to agree, except she didn't want to lie. She, too, missed the closeness they'd once shared in the operating room.

But she missed the closeness they'd shared in and out of the bedroom far more.

"I know what you mean," she hedged. "You were great with Anita." Offering him a fleeting smile, she quickly ducked out of the lounge and headed to the PACU.

Anita was doing wonderfully, clutching her floppy-eared dog, her olive-toned skin pink and healthy.

"She's fine, Dr Howe." Greta sensed her distress. "I promise I'll let you know if anything changes."

"I know you will." Moriah turned away, and went to the OR suite she shared with Blake to find her next patient, Pedro Rodriguez. She didn't have to scrub, but she did put on a new sterile gown, gloves, face mask and bonnet before entering the suite and approaching his bedside. "Hi, Pedro. How are you?"

"Good."

"I'm glad. My name is Dr Howe and I'm going to make sure you are asleep for the surgery." She reviewed his medical record, familiarizing herself with his case. "You're going to feel a pinprick here when I place your IV." She placed the line, then connected fluids to keep the vein open.

A glance at the clock confirmed they were halfway through their day. She'd arrived early, intent on following Blake's wishes of working with one of the other plastic surgeons. But she'd found George Litmann had already assigned her with Blake, probably because they'd worked together in the past. She'd tracked George down, but in the end had been too embarrassed to request a different room assignment. George would have asked why, and she hadn't wanted to delve into her personal history with Blake.

None of that mattered anyway, seeing that Blake had said he liked working with her. She hated to admit it, but she enjoyed working with him as well. Maybe too much. Because every hour they spent together reminded her of the amazing night they'd spent together, followed by a very painful parting.

She tried to tell herself personal feelings weren't the issue here. Professionally, it was far easier to work with someone you knew than with someone you didn't know, especially in less than optimal conditions. Anita's asthma and resulting laryngospasm was a perfect case in point.

For a moment she stared at the dripping IV fluids.

Ironically, in spite of the way he'd hurt her, she f[...] his calm presence in the OR reassuring.

Blake was an excellent surgeon. Working with him was easy. Never once had he pulled any of the theatrics some other surgeons were known for. Teaming up with him in an OR suite reminded her not just of their night together but of the closeness they'd once shared—a friendship she sorely missed.

Could they try their hand at friendship again? She didn't see how, not when the intimacy they'd shared loomed between them like a rocky Peruvian cliff.

Pushing the disturbing, conflicting emotions aside, Moriah smiled down at a drowsy Pedro. Work would help her get over the past. The boy was here for contracture releases of both arms. Burns were common in Peru because of the highly flammable kerosene they used for cooking. Right now Pedro didn't have even gross motor movement of his arms. Once Blake was finished with him, he'd be able to lift and carry objects once again.

"Relax now, Pedro. When you wake up, your surgery will be all finished." She gave him a little more medication until his eyes fluttered shut. "Sleep well, *niño*," she said softly, setting up the necessary equipment to intubate him.

The rest of the OR team entered the room, setting up for the case. One tech doused Pedro's surgical sites with antiseptic solution, then placed sterile drapes around each arm. Moriah concentrated on placing Pedro's endotracheal tube, then setting the proper dose of anesthesia to give him.

She sensed Blake's presence when he entered the OR

suite. He wasn't arrogant, but he was clearly in control of the team. She listened to his voice as he spoke to the scrub techs and nurses, directing them to move several trays, positioning them so he could maximize the room he needed to operate. Since each procedure was different, the room set-up always had to be adjusted accordingly.

There was something right about being here with him, even though she knew this was all they'd ever have. Bittersweet nostalgia filled her heart. They'd fitted together so well professionally.

But not personally, she chided herself. Blake was too much like Ryan, interested in the next female conquest, not caring how many broken hearts he left scattered in his wake.

His husky voice surrounded her as he began to operate, asking for instruments. He had the most amazing hands. Sensitive surgeon's hands. She remembered all too well how his hands had stroked every inch of her body.

Swallowing hard, she glanced at his pensive face and forced herself to admit the truth. No matter what her future held, she still harbored feelings for Blake. They might be twisted, contradictory feelings, but they wouldn't be denied.

If she wanted to succeed in her quest to get over him, she'd better figure out a way to get the mystic allure of Blake Powers out of her system, once and for all.

Moriah took off her gloves and face mask, tossing them aside. They'd spent long hours in the OR, but her day wasn't over yet.

"Do you know Anita's room number?" she asked Greta in the post-anesthesia recovery unit.

"I believe she's in room 201 on the second floor," Greta responded.

"I'd like to check on her before I go home." The little girl she'd performed the tracheostomy on earlier that day had haunted her all day. Normally, she'd make rounds on the post-op patients first thing in the morning, but she couldn't bear to leave without checking on Anita.

Greta smiled, then stifled a yawn. "I'm heading back to the hotel, I just sent my last patient to his room. I can't believe how stoic these people are. Your patient didn't take a single milligram of morphine. And you should have seen his face light up when I gave him the stuffed ostrich." Greta shook her head in amazement.

"I'm surprised Pedro took one of the toys," Moriah commented.

"He said he wanted to take it home for his little brother," Greta explained. "But I suspect he liked the attention, too."

"He's a great kid. Take care, Greta. See you in the morning." Moriah headed down the hall, choosing to take the stairwell to the second floor rather than trust the ancient elevator. She found Anita's room without difficulty. Her mother was sleeping in the chair beside her bed.

"*Hola*, Anita," Moriah whispered, trying not to awaken Anita's mother. "How are you?" She repeated the question in Spanish.

The little girl couldn't smile because of the recent

surgery to her face, but she lifted her hand and showed Moriah the floppy-eared dog she held.

"Oh, I see you still have Floppy." Moriah was pleased to note Anita's skin was pink and warm, indicating she was oxygenating much better and seemingly having no trouble breathing through her tracheostomy tube. "He's adorable, and so are you."

Anita nodded her head and played with the dog, making him jump through the air with her hand, her eyes smiling when his ears flopped up and down.

"I'll come back in the morning to take that tube out of your throat," Moriah told the girl in Spanish. Anita nodded again as if she understood, and Moriah turned to leave.

Nearly bumping face first into Blake, who was lounging in the doorway.

"It's a little late for you to be here, isn't it?" he said by way of greeting.

"For you, too." Working with him throughout the day had stretched her nerves to breaking point. Although she'd focused her energy on her patients, she'd been aware of his constant presence on a deeper level all day. "Excuse me." She made as if to duck around him.

"Wait for me, I'll walk back to the hotel with you." Blake entered Anita's room and bent over to examine the skin flap he'd placed during surgery.

He spoke to Anita and her mother in a deep reassuring tone. Moriah lingered, listening to what he had to say, then realized she was playing right into his hands. There was no reason to wait, not when she had things to do.

Instead of going straight to the hotel, she had planned to stop by and see Rasha. The maternity ward was located on the other side of the hospital, so she headed in that direction, finding Rasha's room without difficulty.

Conscious of possibly invading her privacy, Moriah knocked hesitantly on the door. Rasha bade her enter, so she pushed the door open, and was surprised to find a handsome young man holding the baby.

"*Hola*, Moriah." Rasha greeted her with a smile.

"I hope I'm not interrupting." Moriah edged closer, wanting to get a good look at Rasha's daughter.

"This is my husband, Manuel. He was working out in the fishing boats when the labor pains started. He is happy to see his daughter, but not so happy he missed her birth. He also wasn't happy my mother's car ran out of gas."

Moriah grinned at the way Rasha rolled her eyes. "But at least everything is fine, right, Manuel?"

The dark-haired man flashed her a bright smile and nodded. "Yes, and thank you for being there for Rasha. I know she was more calm because you were there to help."

"I didn't do anything. Rasha is the one who did all the work." Moriah gazed at the infant in his arms. "Your daughter is beautiful. What did you name her?"

"Margarita," Manuel answered, his deep voice filled with awe. "And, yes, she is the most beautiful baby in the world."

Since she'd heard exactly the same sentiment from a few of her siblings about their own children, Moriah had to laugh. "I agree. Well, I won't intrude, I only wanted to stop in to say hi."

"Would you like to hold her?" Rasha asked.

You bet I would. Moriah quickly nodded. Manuel stepped forward and very carefully placed the infant in her arms.

Moriah gazed down at Margarita's perfect, tiny face. A flicker of doubt stabbed her heart. What if she never fell in love with a man who wanted a family like she did? She had learned the hard way with Blake that logic and love didn't necessarily go hand in hand.

When the baby's face scrunched up as if she might cry, Moriah forced the negative thoughts from her mind. "Shh, there now, it's all right," she crooned.

The baby relaxed and, all too soon, she regretfully handed the infant back to her daddy. "I'd better get going."

"Oh, please, come back to visit again tomorrow," Rasha begged. "Soon I'll be discharged home."

"All right, I'll come back soon, I promise." Moriah eased back out of the room, struck by how cozy the three of them were together, the start of their very own family.

A flicker of envy invaded her heart. That closeness was exactly what she'd longed for. What she'd thought she'd discovered with Blake.

Moriah knew her relationship with Ryan had been missing a key element even before he'd broken things off. She hadn't loved Ryan, not the way a woman should love the man she was about to marry. But she should have known better than to think things would be different with his bachelor buddy Blake. Love couldn't surmount all obstacles, and he was as much the antithesis of a family man as Ryan had been.

Stepping outside, she noted darkness had fallen. Blake would already be at the hotel by now. Why had he asked her to wait for him? Hadn't they pretty much agreed to stay out of each other's hair? Maybe Blake thought they could remain friends, despite everything that happened between them.

If so, he needed a major reality check.

"I've been looking all over for you." His deep voice startled her, drawing her from her pensive thoughts when he fell into step beside her. "Where did you disappear to?"

"I went to visit Rasha, met her husband Manuel, and caught a glimpse of her beautiful baby." She slanted him a sidelong glance. "Something I'm sure wouldn't have interested you."

He seemed startled by her accusation. "Rasha was the woman you helped to give birth, right? Why wouldn't I want to meet her?"

She fell silent, knowing she was being unfair. Just because Blake hadn't been interested in a long-term relationship didn't mean he was an ogre. She really had to get over this.

"Are you hungry?" he asked. "We could grab dinner."

She was glad that he'd let the subject drop, but she still said, "No." A lie, since she was indeed famished, but sharing a meal with Blake was right at the top of her list of worst possible things to do. "Thanks anyway."

"Please?" His cajoling tone raked over her taut nerves.

Go away, she wanted to shout at him. *Leave me alone!*

"Stop it," she said sharply. Halting in the street, she swung around to face him "I thought you understood, I'm not in the mood for games. Why don't you find some other woman who would be thrilled at the thought of having dinner with you?"

Blake's face was difficult to read in the darkness. "I'm not trying to play games with you, Moriah." His voice was quiet, serious. "I just think we need to talk."

"There isn't anything to say."

"We've worked together the entire day and managed to get along fine. I think we can manage to share a meal."

Warily, she faced him. The thought of skipping dinner was appealing, especially if it meant spending one more minute alone with Blake, but her stomach rumbled warningly and she knew she wouldn't get any sleep if she went to bed hungry. The curse of a high metabolism.

"Don't skip dinner on my account." Blake accurately read her thoughts. "You need to eat. I'll leave you alone, if you prefer."

"I'm not in the mood for games," she warned him again, stepping past him and leading the way into the hotel dining room.

The place was nearly empty. No such luck as to find any of the team members to use as a buffer. She took a seat across from Blake, trying to remember the last time they'd shared an intimate meal for two.

She glanced at him from beneath her lashes. Being

here with Blake brought back so many memories that it was difficult to remember the reasons why she needed to avoid him. Why was she so torn between the future she longed for and the man who was supposed to be a part of her past?

The waiter arrived to take their order. When he left, an awkward silence fell between them. Moriah racked her brain to come up with some sort of neutral topic of conversation. Work? Their patients?

"I'm sorry," Blake said abruptly.

Caught off guard, she stared at him. "For?"

He met her gaze head on. "Hurting you."

"Really?" She couldn't help her brittle tone. "You didn't think flirting with another woman mere hours after we spent the night together would hurt me?"

He actually winced, as if the memory pained him. "That night together shouldn't have happened. I only wanted to comfort you. I knew you were grieving for Ryan. Hell, we were both grieving for him." He cleared his throat. "We comforted each other that night. Maybe I shouldn't have let things go so far, but I didn't hear you saying no."

His words caused a hollow, helpless feeling to expand in the pit of her stomach.

Because he was absolutely right. Things had gotten way out of control between them.

Except comfort wasn't the reason she'd slept with him that night. She had made love with him because she'd mistakenly believed she'd really loved him.

Her problem, not his.

CHAPTER FOUR

BLAKE'S stomach churned as he watched myriad emotions flit across Moriah's face. Sorrow. Pain. Regret.

Mostly regret. He felt the same thing himself. He'd thought being here with her would help put the past to rest, but so far he'd only managed to make things worse.

He was the one who'd searched for her throughout the hospital. He should have listened to the logical part of his brain that had told him to let her go. Circumstances beyond their control had brought them back to Peru. But what made him think she was at all interested in anything he had to say?

"That night shouldn't have happened." Moriah repeated his words in apparent agreement. She fell silent when the waiter brought their meal and for a tense moment he wondered if she'd leave. But she didn't. Instead, she merely picked up her fork. "I'd prefer to forget my lapse in judgement."

"I don't regret our time together, even if you do." He clenched his jaw, contrarily annoyed with how she'd referred to their night together as a "lapse in judgement."

They'd shared a night of pleasure—it wasn't his fault they both wanted different things out of life. Edgy need for her had ridden him for what seemed like for ever, worse in those months after her breakup with Ryan. Then the news of Ryan's death had reached them on their last night in Peru. All he'd intended had been to offer a shoulder to cry on. Instead, he'd ended up taking advantage of the situation. The moment she'd returned his kiss, he had been lost.

She carefully set down her fork. "I'd rather not talk about it, if you don't mind."

He knew he should leave it alone. But he couldn't. "Is that why you left Trinity Medical Center and joined that private practice across town?"

Moriah raised her hand, signaling the waiter. When he scurried over, she gestured toward her untouched meal. "Would you please wrap this for me?"

The waiter broke into a torrent of Spanish, asking if there was something wrong with the meal. She assured him the food was fine, but she was too exhausted to eat now and needed to return to her room.

"Moriah, don't." Helplessly he watched as the waiter brought her a bag for her food. Ignoring him, she quickly transferred the contents of her plate to the bag.

"We can't rehash the past, Blake." She stood to leave. "I've moved on with my life. And so have you. Maybe you're a man who enjoys the chase, but I'm not willing to run. Good night."

She turned and left the dining room. He stared after her retreating figure, knowing she was wrong.

Maybe once he had enjoyed the chase. But not in the

past year, since spending the night with Moriah. He'd thought flirting would be a way to help him forget about her. But it had failed to work.

He feared nothing would make him forget the tiny slice of heaven he'd experienced in her arms.

Dawn had barely crept over the horizon when Blake arrived at Trujillo hospital. Making rounds, he visited each of his post-op patients from the day before. He was pleased with their progress: everyone was recovering nicely. He spent extra time with Anita's mother, who felt guilty for the role she'd unwittingly played by not confirming Anita's asthma. He understood, and reassured her as best he could, explaining that, in all honesty, the laryngospasms could have happened even if they had known about the asthma, or even if the girl hadn't had asthma. He left, hoping she believed him.

Despite his successful operations, he didn't feel the usual surge of satisfaction. His emotions remained unsettled thanks to the erotic dreams of Moriah that had invaded his sleep all night.

In the harsh light of day, he felt a sharp stab of annoyance. Weakness was something he refused to tolerate. He needed to get his act together, to get his wishy-washy head screwed on straight.

Moriah was just a woman. Heaven knew, there were plenty of them out there. Sure, maybe his days of playing the field were over. Maybe what he needed to do was to find a woman as dedicated to her career as he was to his. Someone who wasn't tethered to the idea of having a big, noisy family.

With a determined step he headed down to the OR suites. His first case of the day was Arturo, the forty-year-old man with extensive face and neck burns who they'd squeezed into the schedule. The procedure would take a good six to eight hours, and he was anxious to begin. He often saw these procedures like puzzles, whose pieces needed to be replaced to be complete.

Per protocol, he scrubbed extensively with antimicrobial solution prior to entering the sterile area. He used the time to clear his mind of his personal problems, thinking instead of the complicated procedure to come.

He found Moriah already in the room, smiling at his patient as she prepared him for anesthesia. Her eyes were bright and lively as she placed the IV catheter and administered a dose of Versed.

"How is Arturo doing?" Blake asked, as he surveyed the sterile instrument trays, grateful to find everything ready.

"He's great, actually. I don't think I've ever seen a patient this excited about having surgery." Moriah's eyes over the rim of her face mask crinkled in a smile. "He was talking a mile a minute, it wasn't easy to calm him down. For a while there I thought I'd need to give him a double dose of medication."

Her words warmed his heart. As much as he'd come on this mission to cover for Ed Granger, he had to admit that assisting people who really needed help was gratifying. Humbling. The people here, men like Arturo, were easy to work with, so compliant with their care compared to some of the people he saw in the US. In many ways he preferred practicing here in Peru.

"Let's get started, then." Blake snapped on a pair of sterile gloves. "I'm ready when you are."

"Give me a few minutes to secure his airway." Moriah deftly intubated the patient and then played with the dials on the anesthesia machine. "All right, he's ready."

Blake quickly became engrossed in the microscopic surgery. At some level he was aware of Moriah reciting the patient's vital signs every hour. Once in a while he paused to stretch when his neck muscles cramped from peering through the microscope. Halfway through the case, he reached the point where he'd planned a short break. The first graft had been placed; the second one still needed to be done.

"Blake? Do you have a minute to come look at this?" George poked his head into the room.

"What's going on?"

"One of the locals needed a crash C-section and the baby has a diaphragmatic hernia. One of our surgeons helped with the infant's surgery, but we need to keep the abdomen open and we don't have any synthetic Gortex mesh to use." George's gaze was troubled. "We brought plenty of regular abdominal mesh, but for this particular case they need something stronger. Come and take a look, maybe you can come up with something we've missed."

"I was just planning to take a break." He glanced at Moriah. "Send someone to give Moriah a break, too."

"I'm all right," she protested.

Blake shook his head. "I need you for the long haul

so don't even think of arguing. Besides, I want you to come look at this newborn with me. Maybe, between the two of us, we'll come up with an idea."

Moriah reluctantly handed over the reins of anesthesia to Terrance, another of the team's anesthesiologists. She and Blake followed George into OR suite five, changing their gowns, masks and hats along the way. In minutes, Blake and Moriah had joined the small group standing around the OR table.

"See? I've tried to use this regular mesh, but it's just not strong enough to give the hernia the stability it needs." Frustration was evident in the surgeon's tone. "I don't know what to do."

Blake frowned at the infant boy's abdomen, trying to think of a solution. Gortex was like thin rubber. What they needed was a rubbery material, something strong enough to hold the infant's intestines in place, yet with a little give to it.

"What about using part of a plastic IV bag?" Moriah suggested.

Of course. Why hadn't he thought of that? "The inside of the bag is sterile, yet the plastic is flexible enough and strong enough to cover the abdominal organs. You know, it just might work."

"I'll get one from the PACU." The circulating nurse darted from the room, returning a few minutes later with sterile scissors and an empty IV bag.

Blake took the items from her and eyed the infant's abdomen, then cut a square from the IV the same approximate size. Handing it to the team, he watched as the surgeon sutured the edges of the plastic in place.

"It's perfect, holding the surgical site with the right amount of firmness. Great idea, Moriah." The surgeon glanced at her. "Thanks."

She smiled. "No problem."

Pride swelled in Blake's chest. He grinned at her. "Let's get something to eat, just for a few minutes."

"Sounds good."

There was an ample supply of juice and crackers in the OR lounge. Blake didn't really want to run all the way down to the cafeteria so the simple nourishment would have to do.

Moriah nibbled on a cracker. "Can you imagine using an IV bag in place of Gortex in the States?" Moriah chuckled. "Someone would try to sue on the grounds the FDA hadn't approved IV bags for that particular use."

"Yeah, it is nice practicing here, without worrying about a zillion senseless regulations," Blake acknowledged. "The US could learn something from Peru."

"I wish."

"Moriah?" Greta entered the break room. "There's a phone call for you, from the US."

"Who is it?" Her eyes widened.

"Your brother, John."

"Is something wrong?" Blake asked, as she hurried off.

"I don't know. He didn't sound upset on the phone." Greta shrugged and turned away.

Blake's thoughts churned as he headed back to the sink outside the OR suite to re-scrub. He'd met Moriah's extensive family a few times over the years and knew they were a close-knit bunch. He and Ryan had mostly stood on the sidelines, feeling strangely isolated as Moriah and her siblings had mercilessly teased each other. As the only child of parents who had hauled him from one obscure country to another until, at the age of five, they had sent him to live with his aunt and uncle indefinitely, he hadn't been able to quite identify with the noisy, rambunctious group.

Not that his unorthodox upbringing meant much now. His parents were long gone, having died in a small plane crash while traveling to a mission.

Moriah's parents, on the other hand, were alive and well, even if they were getting on in years. With a frown he finished scrubbing, hoping there was nothing seriously wrong back home.

"Johnny, I can't believe you called me out of a case to tell me you're getting married." Moriah laughed and shook her head in amazement. "You're lucky I happened to be on break. This call is going to cost you a bundle."

"Sis, I'm killing two birds with one stone here. Mom and Dad have been freaking out because they haven't heard from you."

Guilt flushed her cheeks. "I know, I'm sorry. It's been crazy busy around here. Please, tell everyone I'm fine."

"Will do. Take care of yourself."

"Congrats, John. Tell Elizabeth I can't wait to welcome her into the family." She hung up the phone, smiling wryly.

Her little brother was getting married. Who would have thought? For a while there, he'd seemed to jump from one relationship to another. Just like Ryan. And Blake.

Soberly, she returned to the main OR. As happy as she was for her brother, she wished the thought of John's wedding didn't make her feel so lonely. Her plan to purge the remnants of her feelings for Blake from her system didn't seem to be working very well so far.

A few more days, though, and she was sure she'd have the task mastered.

Steeling her resolve, she donned her sterile garb and hurried into the room.

"Everything all right?" Blake asked, when she took over from Terrance.

"Sure. Everything's fine." She suspected her falsely bright tone didn't fool him in the least.

He stared at her for a long moment, then nodded and turned his attention to work. She reviewed Terrance's notes, familiarizing herself with how her patient had fared in her absence. Eventually, though, she found herself gazing once more at Blake.

The way he managed to perform painstaking surgery for hours on end totally amazed her. In some ways, her job wasn't nearly as hard, although she knew they were equally important. They both had to stay alert and ready for the unexpected for long hours during a case. Why wasn't Blake more arrogant, like some of the other surgeons she worked with? Then maybe it wouldn't be so hard to hang on to her anger toward him.

After they'd finished with Arturo they took another quick break before starting the second patient, a young girl with bilateral lower leg contracture releases. The eight-year-old hadn't walked in two years, since the original burns.

"Louisa's blood pressure is stable, 98 over 62, and her pulse is steady at 102," Moriah recited for Blake's benefit. She knew from working with him in the past how he demanded periodic updates on his patient during the case. Something had happened while he'd been a resident, he'd confided to her last year. One of his patients had taken a turn for the worse during the course of an operation. But the anesthesiologist had simply kept giving stronger and higher doses of medication, rather than telling the surgeons what was going on. They had just about finished the case when the patient had suffered a cardiac arrest. They'd coded him for over an hour, but he'd died. And from that moment on Blake had vowed to practice differently.

His real concern for his patients was just another aspect of his character to admire. The patients weren't statistics to him, numbers that had to be balanced so there weren't too many deaths. They were real people. Over and over again she'd watched him spend a little extra time with his patients, as he had with Anita and her mother.

With a scowl she sought to remember those things about him she didn't like. His penchant for going from woman to woman. The way he seemed to stand completely alone, even in a crowd.

The way he'd walked away from her, as if their night of love-making hadn't meant a thing.

Ryan had mentioned once that Blake had had a rough childhood, but hadn't elaborated on the subject. Watching Blake work, she realized she didn't really know much about his personal life prior to medical school. She did know he was conservative with his money, and he'd once said that he'd been forced to take out several large student loans to get through medical school. But other than those few skimpy facts, she didn't know much at all about his past.

He must have sensed her gaze, because he glanced up at her.

"Louisa's vitals are still stable," she said quickly.

"Good." His eyes crinkled in a smile. Lord, his face was half-covered with his face mask and she still felt his smile all the way to the bottoms of her feet.

The man had dated more women in a year than she had friends, and her pulse still quickened, her stomach tightening when he gave her one of his long, measuring looks.

She needed her head examined, big-time.

"I'm finished here," Blake announced. "Go ahead and reverse her." He pushed the instrument tray out of the way with his foot and pulled off his bloody gloves.

Moriah gave the necessary medication and cut back the general anesthetic. The anesthetic drugs they used now were great. The whole process of waking patients up went much more smoothly and quickly than in years past.

"I'm taking her over to the PACU," she told Blake.

"All right, tell them not to mess with the leg splints I put on her."

"I will." Moriah wheeled her patient down the hall to the PACU and Greta's capable hands. They'd barely gotten her settled when the patient began to flail around on the cart.

"Give her some morphine," Moriah told Greta, attempting to hold the girl down. "She must be in pain."

"All right, here's another two milligrams," Greta told her as she pushed the medication into Louisa's IV.

The poor girl still writhed in the bed, so Moriah lowered her body over the patient's thrashing legs, hoping to protect Blake's surgical sites.

"Give her another dose. Is her IV working? What you gave didn't seem to be touching her." Moriah hoped they hadn't lost the girl's IV.

"You're right, Dr Howe. Her IV isn't working. I'll need to start another line."

Good grief, how could they start another IV when the poor girl was experiencing such pain? "I'll do it. Help me by holding her down."

Louisa continued to buck and flail on the gurney. Starting another IV wasn't easy, although with Greta's help Moriah finally managed to slide the catheter in.

"There, quick, give the morphine. And the Versed," Moriah directed, holding the patient down from her side of the gurney. The medications were on the table beside Greta.

Greta administered the morphine, but not quickly enough. Snap! The sound of a breaking splint echoed through the room like a gunshot. "Oh, my God, call Blake. She just snapped one of her leg splints in two."

Moriah continued to hold her patient and soon, once the medication actually reached her bloodstream, Louisa calmed down. Blake muttered under his breath as he re-created a new splint for her.

"Sorry about that," Moriah apologized. "We should have realized there might be a problem with the IV sooner."

"No harm done to the surgical sites, thank heavens," Blake commented. "I've seen some unruly kids back in the States, but I don't think I've ever seen one of them snap a splint in two." He shook his head in amazement. "I'd like to sit here and watch her for a few minutes. Ask someone to send up a couple of dinner trays."

So much for her plan to avoid spending time with him outside the OR suite. "Do you think that's necessary?" Moriah asked, glancing down at their patient. "She's seems better now. And Greta is here to watch her."

"Greta will be busy when the patient in OR suite four comes out in another five minutes. Besides, I'd rather make sure she's all right for myself, especially since the meds you gave her will soon wear off."

Unable to come up with another argument, Moriah reluctantly sat, as Blake crossed the room and used the wall phone to order a couple of dinner trays. At least this wasn't as bad as sitting across from him in the intimacy of the hotel restaurant.

Greta's presence on the other side of the room was enough of a reminder that they were still at work.

Louisa lay peacefully in her cubicle as they ate their dinner at the main desk.

"Why did your brother call? Are your parents all right?" Blake asked casually.

Feeling foolish, she nodded. "Yes, they're fine. Just worried about me, I guess. I haven't had time to find one of those internet café places to send them a message."

He frowned. "You should have said something. There's a small restaurant with internet access just down the circular road a little ways. I could have taken you over there."

Why was Blake suddenly concerned about her family? Very odd. "That's not the only reason he called. He wanted to let me know he's getting married."

"Married?" Blake's frown deepened. "He's far too young to get married, isn't he?"

She laughed. "He's only two years younger than me, which makes him twenty-nine." To a guy like Blake, forty-nine was probably too young. And her thirty-one suddenly seemed incredibly old, especially if she hoped to have children. "I'm very happy for him. He's thrilled to have found the woman of his dreams."

He paused in the act of lifting his fork to his mouth. "Do you know her well?"

"No, actually, I haven't met her yet." Moriah toyed with the food on her plate. "But I do know that if she loves my brother, she'll fit into the family just fine."

"You don't know that for sure." Blake carefully set his fork down and pushed his plate away, as if he couldn't eat any more. "Some people don't like big families. I hope, for your brother's sake, the woman he's chosen isn't one of them."

"Like you." She hadn't meant to say the words out loud, but the guilt in his eyes only confirmed, with sick certainty, what she already knew.

Blake had seriously meant what he'd once said. He didn't plan to have a family. Ever.

CHAPTER FIVE

"WE'RE not talking about me, but your brother." Blake neatly dodged her comment. "He's the one who needs to be sure."

"I know my brother. He wouldn't ask someone to marry him if he didn't love her." Moriah narrowed her gaze and let out a harsh laugh. "You're hardly the one I'd listen to as an expert on that subject. Trust me, John knows the difference between lust and love."

Despite her tart tone, he didn't get angry, but simply looked at her. One of those long, measuring glances she was beginning to resent because of the way they made her squirm.

"We shared more than lust, Moriah."

Oh, if only that were true. She shook her head, toying with the food on her plate. "No, we didn't."

She heard him sigh. "Just because we want different things from life doesn't mean we weren't compatible in some ways."

So they were just sexually compatible, huh? Now she felt insulted.

"Hey, you two." Greta approached the main desk,

forestalling further argument. "Is there any food left for me? I'm starved."

"Sure, get Blake to order you another tray." Moriah stood, intent on taking her half-eaten tray of food to the dirty-utility room. On her return trip she paused beside their patient's gurney. "I think Louisa is fine now, I'm going to discharge her to a regular room."

Ignoring Blake's penetrating stare, she wrote the discharge orders and left the PACU.

But outside she paused and took a slow, calming breath. Because, though she hated to admit it, deep in her heart she knew his comment had come far too close to the truth.

On her part anyway, she'd felt a lot more than lust for him.

The next day passed in a complete blur. Moriah was scheduled to cover other anesthesiologists for breaks and lunches, which was a good thing, because it was easier to avoid Blake.

We shared more than lust, Moriah.

If that was the case, why had he walked away from her so easily? Not just leaving her, which had been painful enough, but intending to move on to the next woman before the sheets on her bed had grown cold?

At dinnertime, she tried to grab something to eat, but her appetite was gone. Outside, in the circular street, she was surprised to find Henri standing beside a large bus.

"Henri!" She hadn't seen him since that first day in the clinic. "I've been wondering where you were. We'll need your mother's permission before we can get you scheduled for surgery."

The boy ducked his head, as if embarrassed. "I can't. My mother is dead. I live in the orphanage now."

"Oh, Henri." Concerned, Moriah wrapped her arm around his thin shoulders. "I'm so sorry to hear that."

He shrugged. "The orphanage is not so bad. We come to the city sometimes, and that was how I was lucky to find you."

"Yes, and I was lucky to find you, too." Moriah thought fast. "Henri, who is the person in charge at the orphanage? We'll need an adult's consent for you to have surgery."

"Sister Rita is the person in charge, but she's not there today. Sister Eloise is here with us."

She glanced up to see a woman herding a group of laughing kids toward the bus. "Henri, tell Sister Rita I'll be in touch, all right?" Moriah stepped back to allow the kids to pile on the bus. Henri nodded, then climbed aboard with the rest. His face was pressed against the window, watching and waving at her as the bus drew away.

Moriah tried not to worry about Henri as she headed toward the hotel. Although the hour was early, she avoided the dining room, not wanting to run into Blake, and crawled into bed. She didn't set her alarm because, after five days of surgery, tomorrow was her day off. She knew from checking the schedule that Blake had the day off too but, unlike last year, they hadn't made any plans to spend the day together.

She should be relieved at the reprieve.

But she wasn't.

Sleep didn't come easily. She tossed and turned, then tossed and turned again.

Finally, she stared at the ceiling. No point in lying to herself any longer. No matter how stupid it was, she couldn't move on with her life the way she wanted, because her feelings were still stuck on Blake.

The next morning, at the decadently late hour of eight-thirty, Moriah crawled from her bed. Facing her reflection in the mirror over her bathroom sink, she gave herself a little pep-talk. So what if she still had feelings for Blake? The earth wasn't going to stop rotating on its axis over the news. She just needed to find a way to deal with it, at least until they returned home.

And there was no reason to let Blake know how messed up her heart was over him. With a frown, she scrubbed her teeth, as if by wearing away the plaque she'd wear away the doubts. Enough stewing about Blake. She had things to do.

She had chosen not to go on the Inca ruin trip this year, not when the memory of last time, how she and Blake had spent the day together, walking hand in hand while staring in awe at the geometric architecture, remained crystal clear in her mind.

Instead, she'd decided to explore the rocky cliffs overlooking the ocean. The rhythmic waves would soothe her troubled soul and the hot sun would feel great against her skin.

The cliffs weren't dangerous, especially as she wasn't going to be doing any serious rock-climbing.

She wore rugged shoes with her walking shorts and a carry-pouch filled with lip balm, crackers and water. She figured she could grab a big breakfast before she left, then return to the hotel in time for an early dinner.

Breakfast consisted of tortilla-wrapped omelets stuffed with peppers. The food was so delicious she ate to the point she had to wait an additional thirty minutes for everything in her stomach to settle. The tactic worked against her, because when she asked the hotel if she could rent a two-wheeled bike, they were briefly unavailable. In Trujillo, more people rode bikes than drove cars. They promised to obtain a bike for her, though, and within the hour they proudly provided her with one.

As she straddled the bike, preparing to take off, she noticed Blake standing at the side of the street, conversing with one of the locals. For a moment she was tempted to go over to see what he was doing, then berated herself for being so curious. Blake's time off had nothing to do with her. She deliberately settled her bottom on the bike saddle and headed east.

She thought she heard him call her name, but when she glanced back over her shoulder she didn't see any sign of him. His voice must have been in her imagination.

The roads were worn and a little rougher than she was used to, but she enjoyed the ride anyway, feeling exhilarated at simply being outdoors with the wind in her hair and the sun on her face. The salty scent of the ocean was enticing. The beach in Trujillo was crowded at this time of the year and she loved seeing the brightly dressed people *en masse* on the sandy shore.

Rather than join the playful atmosphere on the

beach, Moriah rode her bike to the base of one of the gently sloping cliffs overlooking the ocean. She parked the bike, hiding it behind a rather large outcropping of rock, then began to climb.

She chose an easy path, not seeking thrills but longing to get to the spacious, flat mesa-like top. With her sturdy shoes, the going wasn't difficult. She hauled herself up to the top.

Oh, my. She sucked in a quick breath. What a glorious view. The bright sun glinting off the water, the dark bobbing heads of children playing in the surf. Ignoring the dust, she sat on the ground and wrapped her arms around her knees, resting her chin on them and listening to the sound of rolling waves hitting the shore.

She'd come here to be alone, but she quickly grew tired of her own company. Too bad she hadn't found the courage to invite Blake. Maybe he wasn't the man of her future, but he was a good companion. Last year they'd had such fun spending the day together, it just didn't feel right to be here without him.

Then again, she needed to learn to live her entire life without him. Better get used to that fact.

Moriah had no idea how long she sat there, but eventually she grew hungry. After taking the crackers and water out of her pack, she ate her snack, then decided it was time to climb down to find her bike.

Climbing down was trickier than going up. Not because the sandy rocks were steep, but because of the grooves between the rocks. She wasn't in a hurry, though, so she took her time, testing each foothold carefully before moving downward.

Still, the sand-covered rocks were more slippery than she'd remembered. Unexpectedly, the toe of her right shoe skidded sideways. She clutched the rock for balance, but her attempt to shift her weight failed and her foot shot down into a crevice.

"Ouch!" She yelped as her ankle bone rapped sharply against unyielding rock. For a moment she stayed where she was, struggling against the pain. Awkwardly, she balanced her weight on her hands and tried to lever herself upright.

Her foot wouldn't budge.

She frowned, peering down at her trapped foot. The crevice wasn't deep, but it certainly had enough depth so she couldn't even see the top of her shoe. Her foot was at an odd angle, and already the strain on her ankle was painful. Irritated, she tugged on it again. The darn thing had gone in easily enough, surely it would come out the same way.

Maybe the sole of her shoe was caught on a bit of rock. Wincing, she tried to turn her foot, one way and then the other, but without success. The darned thing wouldn't move even a millimeter.

Now what? She glanced around in search of aid, but there wasn't anyone in sight. All the people on the beach were out of sight, as she'd taken the far side down.

Sitting on the rock wasn't easy, with her stuck foot. And all too soon the pain escalated to a full-blown throbbing.

How could she have been such an idiot? Why had sitting on the top of a cliff to look out over the ocean seemed like such a good idea? How long would she be stuck here until someone found her?

She wished with all her might that she'd asked Blake to come with her today.

A sharp burning pinprick on her ankle had her jerking upright in alarm. Something had bitten her. But what? Frantically, she thought about what little she knew about the desert as she tried to peer down the dark crevice at her foot.

Her stomach rolled when something scuttled from view. Peru's desert was very much like Arizona. Scorpions lived there and their sting was poisonous. No, get a grip. Scorpions were nocturnal creatures, they shouldn't be out in the middle of the day. Although it was dark between the rocks…

She swallowed hard against a rising wave of panic. Spiders? Did poisonous spiders live here? She recalled reading about tarantulas, which were, in her opinion, the creepiest spiders on earth. Yet even if one had bitten her, tarantulas weren't harmful to humans. Still, just thinking about the large hairy things had her yanking on her trapped foot in earnest, not caring when her ankle protested in pain.

She could only pray that whatever had bitten her wasn't venomous.

Blake paced the area in front of the hotel, unable to shrug off the warning itch between his shoulder blades. Moriah wasn't back yet, and he wasn't afraid to admit he was worried.

He took six steps, then turned to take another six

steps in the opposite direction. He'd seen her ride away on a two-wheeled bicycle she had rented from the hotel. But that had been hours ago, nearly ten-thirty that morning. He glanced at his watch for the tenth time in as many minutes. It was nearly three in the afternoon now.

Where could she be?

Maybe he should have asked her to spend the day with him.

Mentally he kicked himself for the lapse. He'd called out to her as she'd started to ride away, but she hadn't heard him. He should have swallowed his pride and followed her.

At least then he'd know where she was.

Of course, she'd been so annoyed with him she would probably have refused to hang out with him anyway.

Unable to stand it for another minute, he hailed a taxi. Searching for her along the side of the road might be futile, but anything was better than sitting around and waiting for her here.

Taxis were abundant in Trujillo, but one was forced to negotiate a fare prior to going anyplace since they didn't have meters. Normally, he would have given the Peruvian driver a run for his money, but he was too worried about Moriah to haggle over the fee for long.

The driver agreed to be of service for an hour. Blake asked him to head east, since that was the direction she'd been headed when he'd last seen her that morning.

"Where does this road lead?" Blake asked the driver in Spanish.

"To the beach."

Cheered by this news, he figured they'd find Moriah in no time.

He'd thought wrong.

There were lots of people leaving the beach by this time of the day. He instructed the taxi driver to park along the main road, but after fifteen minutes he still didn't see any sign of Moriah.

With a frown he stared at the beachfront. What would Moriah have done? Parked her bike and wandered along the beach, paddling in the waves? He didn't see anyplace where she could safely park the bike without worrying about someone mistaking it for their own. No, the longer he thought about it, the more convinced he was she wouldn't have joined the crowd on the beach.

The rocky cliff caught his eye and he imagined she would have loved sitting up there, enjoying the view. Last year, when they'd gone on the Inca ruin trip, she'd wanted to climb the pyramid, but it hadn't been allowed. He leaned toward the taxi driver.

"Take me to those rocky cliffs over there."

The driver shrugged and turned the yellow cab around, then took a less-traveled side road toward the cliffs.

The flash of metal caught his eye and Blake asked the driver to stop. There, partially hidden behind a rock, was a bike.

"Moriah?" Blake climbed from the cab, calling her name. "Moriah? Are you here?"

"Blake?" He hurried toward the welcome sound of her voice. "Blake! I'm stuck. Please, help me."

"Stuck?" What did she mean? Then he saw her, hanging on, halfway down the rocky slope, with one foot buried in a crevice between two rocks. "OK, I'm coming."

"I've almost got it, I think." She was covered with dust and her clothes were damp with sweat, half-stuck to her skin. He had the wildest urge to kiss her. "If you could just pull, I'm sure it'll come free."

"What is this goopy stuff on your shoe?" He reached down between the rocks to pull gently on her foot.

"Lip balm. I thought maybe if I could lubricate my shoe, I'd be able to yank my foot out."

He felt around the edge of her shoe, trying to find the spot where it was jammed the worst. The lip balm she'd smeared around her foot helped, because with a few tugs he was able to get it free.

She cried out in pain when he eased her foot out from the crevice. Immediately he understood why. Moriah's ankle appeared bruised and swollen.

"I hope it's not broken. This looks painful, Moriah." His concerned gaze met hers.

She tried to smile. "Yeah, but I don't care. I'm just so glad to see you. I had horrible visions of spending the night up here."

He wanted to haul her into his arms, but first things first. "All right, let's get you down without falling." He glanced around, trying to strategize. He'd gotten her foot free, but they weren't off the rocky slope yet.

"I won't fall." Her tone rang with grim determination. "I'm going the rest of the way down on my butt."

True to her word, she used her good foot, both hands and her bottom, and slowly made her way from one rock to the next. He couldn't do anything more than stay nearby in case she slipped.

When she was close enough to level ground, he stopped her with a hand on her shoulder. "Wait here, I'll get down so I can carry you the rest of the way."

"All right." It was telling that she didn't argue with him.

He jumped down and then turned to face her. Reaching up, he put his hands on her waist.

"Reach down and brace your hands on my shoulders," he instructed her. "When I count to three, let yourself slide down toward me. One, two, three."

He braced himself for her weight, then, trying not to bump her injured ankle, carefully set her on the ground. But he didn't let go. Instead, he tightened his grip as relief washed over him.

"Hell, Moriah. You worried me when you didn't come back."

"Oh, Blake." She didn't resist his embrace—in fact, just the opposite. Maybe it was mostly because of her injured ankle, but she leaned heavily against him, burying her face in his neck. "I kept wishing you were with me."

"I wish I'd been with you, too." He lifted her chin with one finger, just enough to capture her startled mouth in a deep, grateful kiss.

CHAPTER SIX

BLAKE lost himself in the sweet softness of Moriah's mouth, memories dive-bombing him from all directions. He couldn't seem to get enough, as if she were the essence of life, what he needed to breathe. Her arms wrapped around his neck, her body soft and pliable against his. The months they'd spent apart fell away as if they hadn't existed. No one felt right in his arms except Moriah.

She pressed urgently against him, as if she was desperate to be closer. His arms tightened around her and the errant thought flashed in his mind that it would be a cold day in Peru before he'd let her go.

"Hey, mister, your hour is up."

"What?" Reluctantly, Blake raised his head to blink at the taxi driver, who'd come to find out what was taking so long. As much as he didn't want to leave, he had to get Moriah off her ankle and back to the hotel. "We're coming. And don't worry, I'll double your fee."

Moriah eased her arms from his neck, then grabbed his sleeve with a sharp hiss. "Uh-oh, my ankle didn't like that. I'll need to hang onto you."

Now that they were on level ground, he was free to

do what he'd wanted all along. "A better idea is to carry you."

"Blake!" she shrieked as he lifted her up. "Don't be ridiculous. I can walk with a little help."

He ignored her protest, unwilling to break the close hold he had on her. Maybe she wasn't badly hurt, but his heart still hadn't quite settled in his chest from her disappearing act. Thank heavens he'd found her.

"Wait! Don't forget my bike." Her voice rose in agitation.

He waited until he reached the cab, then gently set her down. "I won't forget." He pulled the passenger door open behind her. "Can you get in?"

"I'm hardly dying, it's only a sore ankle." She easily folded herself into the cab seat, sliding across until she met the other side.

The cab driver had already fetched her bike. Blake helped to wedge the bulky frame into the trunk, then climbed into the cab beside Moriah. Carefully, he lifted her sore ankle into his lap and began to inspect the damage.

"Bruising, abrasions and swelling." He frowned. "I think I'll have the driver take us straight to the emergency department at the hospital."

To his surprise, she didn't argue, which only convinced him she was in more pain than she let on.

"Do you see any sign of a bug bite?" she asked, resting her head back against the window.

"Bug bite?" He turned her leg gently from side to side. Then he saw it, a circular mark with a halo-like red swelling surrounding the center. His gut tightened with dread. "What bit you?"

"I don't know." She gnawed her lower lip and shrugged. "I couldn't see, but I definitely felt a sharp stinging pain."

"Looks like a spider bite." He searched his memory. What sorts of spiders did they have here?

"Better than the sting of a scorpion, I guess."

"Scorpions are nocturnal," he replied automatically.

"I know, I know." Moriah sighed. "I told myself the same thing. But they do live in rock crevices and it was dark down there. What if I woke one up when my foot slid into the crevice? Maybe he was mad I invaded his turf."

Her light tone belied the dark fear in her eyes, and Blake felt a ripple of concern, unable to discount her theory. "How long ago did you feel the bite?"

"Just before you came. Ten minutes, I'd say, maybe less."

"Long enough that I'd think you would already be feeling the poisonous effects if the culprit was a scorpion." Blake reached over, took her wrist in his and began to assess her pulse. "How is your breathing? Any shortness of breath?"

"No, I'm fine." Her smile was lopsided. "I don't think I like being a patient."

"I'm not too crazy about it myself." Blake was reassured by her steady heartbeat. "Do you have a headache? Dizziness?"

"Maybe just a little headache from being in the sun so long." Moriah reached down to rub her ankle.

"Nothing like the ache in my ankle. And no dizziness."

The taxi driver pulled up at the hotel. Blake leaned forward and tapped him on the shoulder. "Down the road, please, to the hospital. She needs to see a doctor."

The driver muttered something under his breath and pulled off again.

"You are a doctor," she pointed out.

Hell, at the moment his emotions were so involved, he figured he was thinking more like a concerned family member than a doctor. Surely, if something poisonous had bitten her, they'd know by now. He clutched her hand in his.

The thought of losing her made him feel sick.

Living without her was easier to bear when he knew she was healthy and safe. He needed to believe she'd be fine.

Although keeping his distance would be much harder after that heart-stopping kiss.

Moriah grimaced at the need for a wheelchair but she sat without protest. She was afraid if she didn't, Blake would threaten to carry her again.

His gallant gesture had thrown her off balance, literally and figuratively. She'd felt vulnerable yet cherished in his arms. She was so glad he'd found her. Using the lip balm as lubricant had started to work, and her foot had moved slightly when she'd pulled. But even if she'd gotten unstuck to crawl down the rocks, she had no idea how she would have managed to get on her bike to ride all the way back to the hotel.

Blake pushed her wheelchair into the ER. The same young doctor who'd delivered Rasha's baby came toward her. Unfortunately, she hadn't gotten his name, but she forced a smile. "Hello. Remember me? I was the one who brought in Rasha just in time to have her baby?"

His eyes widened in recognition. "Yes, I do. You are a doctor, too, no?"

She nodded. "Dr Moriah Howe. This is Dr Blake Powers."

He bowed at Blake. "I'm Dr Enrique Sanchez. So tell me what has happened."

She gestured to her swollen foot. "It's nothing, really. Fell in the rocks and twisted my ankle."

"She'll need oblique and lateral X-rays to make sure it's not broken," Blake commented from behind her.

Enrique nodded. "I concur. Let's get her into a room first, and take her vital signs. Then we'll order the films."

Moriah didn't appreciate the way they talked around her, as if she wasn't there. Blake pushed her into one of the cubicles and she set the wheelchair brakes so he couldn't push her anyplace else. Before she could open her mouth, though, Blake continued.

"Look at this bite here." He pointed to the affected area on her ankle. "Her foot was wedged between two rocks and she couldn't see what bit her. What sort of native spiders do you have here? Anything poisonous?"

"I can give him the details of what happened without your help, Blake." Moriah was grateful for his rescue, but now she was starting to feel overwhelmed by his presence and she didn't like it one bit. "I'm sure it's just a spider bite."

"The only thing to worry about here are the scorpions," the ER doctor agreed. He knelt at her foot to examine it more closely. "This doesn't look like the sting of a scorpion. And she'd already be very sick, the poison spreads fast."

"Good, that's exactly what we thought." She smiled in relief, then held up a hand. "And if it was a spider that bit me, I don't want to know which kind."

Enrique's small smile spread wider. "You don't like spiders?"

She shivered, trying not to imagine something big and hairy crawling up her leg. "No."

The ER nurse came in and took her vital signs then confirmed the need for X-rays. Moriah tried to be a good patient, but it wasn't easy. First they turned her ankle this way and that, causing shooting pains to dart into her foot, then they wrapped the entire thing in ice. The coolness should have felt good, but all too soon the cold intensified the ache.

Half an hour later she found herself back in the ED. Enrique and Blake were reviewing her films and discussing the possibilities. Her irritation mounted.

"Don't you think you should be showing those to me?"

"Ah, yes. Of course." Enrique nodded and pulled her wheelchair closer so she could see the films as well. "The good news, no broken bones. Just a bad sprain."

"No hairline cracks either," Blake agreed. 'So you'll need to — '

"I know. Rest, ice, elevation." She was well aware of the routine treatment of a twisted ankle. Hobbling around with a bad ankle was going to drive her crazy, though.

"Crutches." Enrique gestured to a nurse, who fetched the crutches. "You will use these for a few days then, when the swelling goes down, you can walk on it."

She eyed the crutches warily. "Are they really necessary?"

Blake came up behind her and dropped his hands on her shoulders. "If you'd rather not use the crutches, I can carry you where you need to go."

"Very funny." She scowled at him over her shoulder, then sighed. "The crutches are fine."

"I asked him to order some painkillers for you, too," Blake added.

She ground her teeth together in frustration. "Thanks, but a little ibuprofen will probably do the trick."

"Use them at night, so you can get a good night's sleep," he advised.

"If I need them." She reluctantly took the small container of pills from him, realizing he was probably right. Despite her bad ankle, she'd still need to work her shifts at the hospital, which would be easier after a good night's sleep. Her annoyance was more as a result of the situation than of Blake's well-meaning concern.

"All right, you are ready for discharge." Enrique handed her the crutches. "Please, come back to see us if the pain gets worse."

"I will." Moriah pulled herself upright and tested out the crutches. They weren't too bad, and it was nice to be self-sufficient.

"Can you make it back to the hotel?" Blake asked. "Or do you want me to call a cab?"

"I can walk, it's only a few blocks." She set off at a brisk pace, then she abruptly stopped. "Oh, no, we forgot my bike in the taxi."

"No, I paid the driver to drop it off at the hotel." Blake shook his head. "You're awfully worried about that bike."

"I had to practically sign over my passport to rent it." Moriah set off again. "Did I thank you for coming to my rescue?"

"Yes, you did." Blake, walking by her side, hesitated for a moment. "I'm glad I came when I did. If you had stayed there much longer, the stress could have broken the bone."

"I do appreciate your help."

In seemingly record time they reached the hotel. Moriah double-checked to make sure her bike had been returned and the hotel manager assured her that everything was fine.

She turned back to Blake. "I'm going to head to my room, I need to get cleaned up."

"Sounds good. Take care of yourself." As if they hadn't shared that amazing kiss, he set off in the opposite direction toward his own room.

Dazed and somewhat disappointed, Moriah watched him leave. With a sigh she sought the sanctuary of her room. What was wrong with her? Why did she have this deep desire for Blake's comfort and company? Nothing had changed. Blake was still the wrong man for her. Spending more time with him wasn't going to change that.

She stripped and tossed her sweat-stained clothes in the corner. They would need to be laundered, a service the hotel provided.

The incident on the rocks had frightened her more than she'd wanted to admit. It was bad enough to get into such a stupid predicament, but worse when you were in a strange country. She hadn't been able to believe her eyes when she'd seen Blake standing there. When he'd caught her in his arms she'd reveled in his reassuring strength, the musky male scent of him filling her head. His hungry kiss had reminded her of the passion they'd shared.

She lingered in the tiny shower. Memories tucked away long ago surged to the forefront. They'd made love with intense abandon, including right here in one of these minuscule showers, exploring the depths of passion between them. Blake had been extremely generous, in both his love-making and in listening.

Until the next morning, when she'd found him at the airport, chatting cozily with Suzanne, one of the nurses. When she'd walked over to greet him, he'd barely spared her a glance, all his concentration focused on the laughing woman beside him.

The memory stabbed her like a knife. Although the fault was really her own. She'd known from the very beginning that Blake was just like Ryan. The two of them had been best friends, bachelor buddies. He'd never promised her anything more than a single night of pleasure.

Rinsing the shampoo from her hair, she tried to shove the memories aside. Resurrecting the past wouldn't help. So what if he'd delivered on his promise for pleasure, then moved on?

She stepped awkwardly from the shower, favoring her right ankle, and dried off with the white fluffy towels. Using the dreaded crutches, she hobbled to the phone to request a tray be brought up. She wasn't really all that hungry, but made an effort to eat.

When she'd finished eating, she found herself at a loose end. She'd changed into a loose-fitting sundress, but staring at the four walls of her room was driving her batty. Too many memories, either from the past or from her recent harrowing experience, kept her from finding relaxation.

Maybe she'd look for that restaurant Blake had mentioned, the one with internet access, and send a few messages home. Filled with purpose, she stood, hobbled with the crutches to her dresser and grabbed a sweater, then headed toward the door.

When she opened it, though, her eyes widened as she found Blake standing on the other side.

"Hi." He shoved his hands into the pockets of his casual cotton pants, his light hair damp from a recent shower. "I, er, wanted to check on you. To make sure you were all right."

"I'm fine." She leaned the bulk of her weight on her crutches and they stood there for an awkward moment.

"I see you're headed out," Blake murmured. "Would you mind some company?"

Her first instinct was to refuse, to protect herself from making the same mistakes all over again.

"Please?"

His quiet plea dissolved her resistance, and she drew a shaky breath and nodded. Maybe this was a mistake, but she couldn't shake the thought of giving this thing between them a chance, to see where it might lead.

She swung through the doorway on her crutches, knowing as she did that she was crossing the threshold into uncharted territory.

CHAPTER SEVEN

BLAKE momentarily lost his breath when Moriah stepped forward, then leaned on her crutches to close the door firmly behind her. Her citrus scent clouded his brain. She wore a loose-fitting dress and while he figured she'd chosen it for comfort, the garment only enhanced her incredibly sexy aura. He knew full well the luscious curves and sleek skin hidden by the fabric, and he longed to unwrap her like a birthday present. Except the date wasn't even close to his birthday. It took all his willpower not to pounce on her like a lunatic.

Seeking control, he cleared his throat, yet was unable to tear his gaze from the enticing picture she made. "So. Where are you headed?"

"I need to find internet access. You mentioned there was a place offering the service right down the street." She gracefully swung her crutches down the hall toward the hotel lobby. "I want to send a message home."

Of course she did. A woman like Moriah would always need her family ties. He understood, even if he couldn't really relate. With an effort he pulled himself together, trying to ignore the clamoring need burning his gut, and nodded. "I'll show you where it is."

"Sure, if you like," was her offhand response.

Moriah was more than self-sufficient enough to find the way by herself, but he felt compelled to tag along anyway.

He fell into step beside her and they walked outside and turned left down the unique circular street. The air was a tad cool, and she shivered a little when the breeze brushed her bare arms. It took every ounce of willpower he possessed not to haul her into his embrace, to warm her body with his.

"Oh, look at the pretty lanterns hanging above the statue." Moriah paused, glancing around in surprise. "Hey, someone's hung ribbons from all the wrought-iron fences, too. Red, blue and pink. It looks as if they're planning a party."

"There's a Trujillo Festival being held at the end of the week," Blake told her. "It's not nearly as big as the Fall Festival known worldwide, but it should be fun."

"How did you hear about the festival?"

"The locals filled me in while I helped them hang lanterns."

"You hung lanterns?" Moriah's eyes widened. "Working on your day off?"

He shrugged. "Why not?"

"Then you wasted another hour looking for me." Moriah's lips curved in a wry smile. "I bet this was the worst day off you've ever had."

"Not even close." Kissing Moriah had more than made the day worthwhile. "My only regret is not spending the entire day with you." The confession slipped out before he could guard his tongue.

"Oh, Blake. I spent the day people watching and listening to the ocean, but the whole time I wished you were with me, too." Her dazzling smile warmed his heart.

Considering he was a man who didn't want the ties of a family, he couldn't understand why he persisted in spending time with her. Yet he couldn't bring himself to leave her either.

They found the internet café-restaurant and Moriah eagerly sat at a terminal, entered her credit-card number then went online. Blake pulled up a chair next to her and watched.

"Don't you want to send a message?" she asked, typing furiously. "I'm sure your parents would appreciate hearing from you."

"My parents are dead." He instantly wanted to kick himself for telling her so bluntly. But, then again, maybe if she understood where he was coming from, he could explain himself, and somehow make amends for the way he'd treated her last year.

The clicking noises stopped and she turned toward him, her dark gaze full of concerned compassion. "Blake, I'm sorry. I didn't know."

He shrugged, uncomfortable with her sympathy. "It's not a big deal. I hadn't seen either of them in years."

Her eyes widened. "But why?"

Damn, he never should have started this whole conversation. He shifted in his seat, wishing he'd followed his original instinct to leave her alone. But he hadn't been able to stay away.

Not even knowing it was for her own good. And for his own sanity.

"They aren't like your parents, Moriah," he finally told her. "They dedicated their lives to their missionary work. I was actually born in Africa. They kept me with them until it was time for me to go to school, then they shipped me off to live with my aunt and uncle. They didn't want kids."

"How awful for you." She reached out and grasped his arm. "I'm sorry, Blake. No parent should ever treat their child like that."

The flesh of his arm burned beneath her touch and he couldn't stop himself from covering her slight hand with his. "Not all families are like yours, Moriah. That's what I was trying to explain to you the other day. Some people aren't made for family life."

"But you could be, if you wanted to."

He slowly shook his head. "But that's the point. I don't want to. Is it a crime to dedicate my life to my career? I tried to make a commitment once, during medical school, but luckily I came to my senses before doing anything disastrous. I don't have a lot of experience with kids, but I do know they take a ton of time and energy that I don't want to give. I'm simply not wired the same way you are."

"I refuse to believe that."

Before he could try to convince her, the door to the café opened and two laughing American women walked in. His heart sank as he recognized Claire and Greta.

"Hi, Moriah, Blake." Greta greeted them enthusiastically. "Isn't this the greatest place?"

"Yes, I'm glad we found a way to get a message home," Moriah agreed, sliding her hand from his. "Much better than a silly postcard."

"Hello, Blake." Claire stepped forward, her sunny smile fading when she noticed Moriah pull her hand from his. With a wounded grimace, she turned away.

He clenched his jaw, but didn't know what to say. He'd barely spoken two words to Claire since the dinner they'd shared that first night. Having a simple meal together shouldn't have meant so much to her. It wasn't his fault they didn't mesh.

Or maybe it was. How many times had he tried to find someone else? Anyone who might make him forget the woman seated beside him?

Damn. He didn't want his head messed up with Moriah.

He stared blindly at the computer screen in front of him. The two nurses moved away, choosing vacant chairs on the opposite side of the room to go online and e-mail messages to their family and friends.

It was a sad commentary on his life that he didn't have a single person he needed to communicate with.

"I'll check my work e-mail while you finish up," he said to Moriah. Work was his life, he needed to remember that. He refused to make the same mistakes his parents had made. He preferred to dedicate his life to his career, a choice he didn't regret. He wasn't so sure he even liked children. The ones he'd met while visiting Moriah's family had been loud and annoying—one had even thrown spit-balls at him.

His heart shouldn't be heavy just because he'd been honest with her. Some people didn't belong in that life.

He was one of them.

She silently stared at him for a long moment, then turned her attention to her computer. She busied herself with sending her messages, then finally turned back to him.

"I'm finished."

"Good." He quickly disconnected his work e-mail, unable to dredge up much interest in the latest healthcare news and hospital politics. "I'll walk you back to the hotel."

Outside, Moriah paused. "I noticed Claire seemed upset with you."

"She doesn't have a reason to be upset. We talked a little and shared dinner once. End of story." He couldn't help his harsh tone.

"You don't say goodbye very well, do you?" Moriah observed, before walking down the street, back in the direction from which they'd come.

Touché. She'd scored a direct hit. He hastened to catch up with her. "I'm sorry."

"For what?" She barely spared him a glance, keeping up a brisk pace with her crutches as if she couldn't get back to the hotel fast enough.

"For leaving you like I did last year." Guilt almost made the words stick in his throat.

"Oh. That." They had arrived at the hotel, and she

turned back to face him. "You know, Blake, I'm sorry, too. Because that night was very special."

The layer of guilt coating his throat thickened. "Moriah—"

"Don't," she interrupted him. "I understand a little better now why you hold people at arm's length. Let's just focus on remaining friends. Good night, Blake."

He didn't want to leave, not like this. There was so much more he should say, so many transgressions to make up for. But he couldn't do it. It was bad enough he'd wanted her for what seemed like a lifetime.

If she ever came to him again, he wasn't sure he would have the strength and the willpower to let her go.

Moriah watched as Blake turned and walked away, an action he'd perfected over the years. She should have been content to let him walk out of her life.

But she had to bite her lip to stop herself from calling him back.

She kept seeing him as a little boy, being shipped off to live with strangers, even if those strangers had been related by blood. Being abandoned at such a young age must have been very hard and explained the aura of isolation she'd noticed about him. Really, though, his background only reinforced what she already knew.

Like Ryan, he was a man who avoided commitment. Or, rather, relationships that might lead to a commitment.

And having a family was the greatest commitment of all.

In the bathroom she splashed liberal amounts of cold water on her face in an effort to quell her overheated hormones. Still, after she'd crawled into bed, sleep eluded her. The enigma of Blake wouldn't leave her alone.

She squeezed her eyes shut, but the images still came. Blake's mouth, hot and needy on hers. His strong surgeon's hands, stroking her breasts, her stomach, the cleft between her thighs. Like a spontaneous combustion, passion had exploded between them.

She'd fallen in love with him that night. And he'd walked from her arms to another woman. In all honesty, he'd treated her with the same casual indifference he'd shown Claire earlier.

When would she learn? The number-one rule in dating men was you couldn't go into a relationship thinking you could change them.

Yet that was exactly what she'd started to believe. She certainly hadn't been at her smartest today. Falling on the rocks, then starting to believe there could be some sort of future between her and Blake.

She might be professionally smart, but on a personal level she had a few things to learn.

Disjointed, illogical dreams prevented her from getting much sleep. Spiders kept invading her room, then Henri was talking to her, explaining about his life in the orphanage, then he morphed into an adult version of Blake, who ignored her to focus his attention on the blonde nurse clinging to his arm. When she confronted him, he patiently explained he didn't love her because she was afraid of spiders.

She woke exhausted, crawled to the edge of her bed, then sat, holding her head in her hands. Heavens, her head hurt, as if her brain cells had worked several hours' overtime, trying to make sense of her dreams. Forcing herself upright, she tested her ankle on the floor. It hurt but, surprisingly, not quite as badly as yesterday. Using the crutches, she shuffled toward the bathroom. A long, hot shower helped erase the cryptic messages etched on her subconscious. Thank goodness Freud wasn't around to analyze her, he'd have a grand time delving into her psyche, she was sure.

She couldn't do anything about Blake, but she could help Henri. Before heading over to the hospital, she decided to see if Terrance would be willing to cover her morning surgeries. All she needed was a few hours to get in touch with someone from Henri's orphanage. It was really early, barely six, so she gathered her courage and called Terrance's room.

"Hello?" His gruff voice only increased her guilt.

"Terrance, it's Moriah. I'm sorry to bother you, but I need a favor. Will you cover for me, just for a couple of hours?"

"Uh, yeah. Sure. I'm on to cover lunches and breaks anyway." He groaned, and she imagined he was crawling out of bed. "Give me a few minutes, and I'll head over to the hospital."

"Great. Thanks, Terrance. I owe you one."

"Yeah, and don't think I won't collect that debt."

Moriah grinned at his threat. "No problem." She hung up the phone, wondering why she couldn't find a guy like Terrance to get hung up on. He was good-looking, nice, and didn't seem to be anti-family.

Although the idea entered her mind that loving

Blake might be worth giving up her dreams of a family.

She caught her breath. No, she couldn't do it.

Pushing aside her incessant thoughts, she focused on the present. Wishing Blake was different was useless. She might love him, but he'd made it clear he didn't love her. Better to concentrate on helping Henri.

Her mission to find someone to grant consent for Henri's surgery took longer than she'd thought it would, but after several phone calls and transfers to various people she finally had it. Sister Rita had raved about Henri, singing his praises for being such a good boy at the orphanage. Apparently, the older kids were responsible for helping out the younger ones and Henri was her pride and joy. Sister Rita was more than willing to give consent for his surgery, especially when Moriah promised to pick him up, saving the woman a trip to the city.

"Come for a visit, *señorita*," the woman urged her. "Henri would love to see you."

"I will," she promised.

Satisfied with her progress, Moriah returned to Trujillo hospital to relieve Terrance. The moment she entered the OR suite, she could sense Blake wasn't himself. A frown marred his brow and he seemed tense. Was this case more difficult than the others?

Blake was already in the middle of his second surgical case and Terrance was more than happy to turn the care of the patient over to her. While listening to Terrance update her on the patient's condition, she heard Blake snap at the circulating nurse because she'd brought the wrong instrument tray.

She glared at him as the poor woman scuttled from the room to fetch the correct tray. His bad attitude was uncharacteristic and, in her opinion, uncalled for. She sent him a dark frown, but he ignored her as he turned back to his patient.

Sebastian was a seventeen-year-old boy with left-sided burns on his arm and leg. After taking a seat at the patient's head, she announced the vital signs for Blake's benefit.

"Sebastian is doing great. His heart rate is 82, blood pressure good at 106 over 70, pulse ox 99 per cent."

"It's a good thing he's doing well, because we're already behind schedule." Blake's cutting tone reinforced his displeasure. "No thanks to your disappearing act this morning."

"I didn't disappear, I had things to do. And Terrance was here."

"Yeah, well, there were things to do here, too."

"Are you trying to tell me Sebastian's care was compromised because Terrance provided his anesthesia?" She wasn't about to listen to such nonsense. Blake remained silent, probably realizing how ridiculous he sounded. With a sigh Moriah settled in her seat and tried to change the subject. "After this case, I'd like to review the surgery schedule with you. I managed to get consent for Henri's surgery."

"Hmm." The circulating nurse brought the replacement tray for Blake to use. He nodded, confirming that this time she'd found the right one, then went to work, concentrating his efforts on releasing the bad contracture in Sebastian's left arm.

Moriah didn't push for an answer, knowing there would be plenty of time for them to discuss Henri's surgery later. She'd only mentioned it in the first place to distract him from his bad mood.

Besides, she already knew exactly which time slot she wanted for Henri. Sister Rita, as the person in charge of the orphanage, had consented to the surgery, but she'd made it clear she couldn't provide Henri the care he'd require during his hospital stay. Moriah had assured the woman she'd take care of everything, and figured she could rearrange her schedule to do that. Since her next day off was two days from now, on Monday, she needed Blake to do the surgery on Sunday evening.

Hopefully, he wouldn't mind. The Blake she knew wasn't the type to hold a grudge, at least not when patient care was involved. Heck, if either one of them deserved to hold a grudge, she did.

"Bring the light closer, please. I need a clear path to visualize the artery clearly for this resection," Blake told the circulating nurse.

"Vitals are still stable," Moriah informed him.

"Good." He blew out a breath and bent over the surgical site. Without warning, the entire OR suite went black.

Everyone in the room froze as a strange, unnatural silence filled the air.

"What the hell?"

Moriah heard Blake's voice in the darkness but she was already feeling for the ambu-bag so she could give manual breaths to her patient. There were no windows in the OR, so the lack of light was absolute. She couldn't even see a shadow.

"Dammit! Where in the hell is the back-up generator?" Blake had every reason to be more than a little annoyed.

"I don't think they have one." Moriah gave Sebastian several deep breaths with the ambu-bag. She wished she could see Blake's face. "The power will come back on any second, I'm sure."

"It had better. For God's sake, I had a scalpel in this kid's arm." His frustration was palpable and she could only imagine how he felt. As if the delicate surgery wasn't difficult enough, without losing power at the worst possible moment.

"This happened last year, too, remember?" Moriah strove to remain calm. "It didn't take long for them to get the power back on."

Luckily, just then the lights flickered on and the familiar hum of the anesthesia machine filled the room. The clock confirmed the power had only been out for three and a half of the longest minutes of her life. Moriah sighed in relief.

Until she noticed Sebastian's dangerously low vital signs.

"Blake, his blood pressure is down to 74 systolic and his pulse ox is only 78 per cent." She unclamped the IV fluids, allowing them to flow wide open into the patient. "Something's happened. We're losing him."

"He's bleeding profusely. I must have nicked the artery when the power went out." Blake's horrified tone confirmed her worst fears. "Get me some suction, I need to see if I can repair the damage."

"I need several units of blood—what type is he?"
Moriah quickly flipped through his chart. When she
found the information, her heart sank. "AB neg? Do we
even have any AB negative blood available?"

"I'll check." The circulating nurse hurried out.

Helplessly, Moriah stared at the monitor. She'd increased his oxygen, bringing his pulse ox up to a whop-
ping 83 per cent, but that wasn't good enough. She
pulled more IV fluids off the cart and hung them on a
pressure bag to get the fluid in as fast as possible.

"I've repaired the artery, but he lost a good liter of
blood." Blake's concerned gaze met hers. "If there isn't
enough blood on hand, we'll need to start asking the
staff for direct donations."

Moriah nodded. "I'm O neg, I'll donate a pint first."

Blake shook his head. "I'd rather you waited. I need
you here. He's better off with blood from a direct AB
negative match."

"O neg is the universal donor," she argued. "I know
there is still a potential reaction to antibodies, but it's
worth the risk." The odds of one of the staff being AB
negative were slim, since it was the rarest blood type of
all.

Blake met her gaze, then nodded. "I know."

The circulating nurse returned with a bag in hand.
"We don't have any AB negative blood. I do have one
unit of O negative blood, but that's all."

"That's not enough." As she spoke, she quickly hung
the single unit of life-saving blood. "Is there anyone
working out there with O negative or AB negative blood
type?"

The nurse shook her head. "No, I already asked."

"Fine. Get Terrance back in here to cover me. I'm going to donate a unit myself."

CHAPTER EIGHT

BLAKE felt a strong sense of admiration as he watched Moriah hand over Sebastian's care to Terrance Whitney before she left the OR suite.

He wished she didn't have to do it, especially since the situation was his fault. He didn't know why he was surprised at her willingness to help, though, because Moriah was the type of doctor to go all the way for her patients.

She didn't try to kill them by slicing their arteries with a scalpel when the power went off. He shook his head. He didn't think he'd flinched, but he must have done to slice the artery like that.

Numb with guilt, he stared down at the open incision in front of him. The repaired artery was holding well, but he still needed to finish the contracture release. When he reached for forceps, he realized his hands were shaking. With a muttered curse he dropped the instrument and resisted the urge to shove the instrument tray across the room.

"Do you have a recent set of vitals for me?" Blake couldn't help his sharp tone. This was a crisis. Whitney should know enough to fill him in on what his patient was doing without being asked.

"Blood pressure marginal at 82 over 45. Pulse remains tachy at 121. His pulse ox is still low at 84 per cent."

"Have you given the entire unit of O negative blood yet?" Blake wanted to know.

"Yeah."

Damn. He'd hoped the blood would help more. He frowned. "Do we have any fresh frozen plasma we can use as a volume expander until we get more blood?"

"Look, I know my job, Powers. I've already given one unit of fresh frozen, with another ready to go." Whitney's clipped tone betrayed his annoyance.

Blake bit back a sarcastic response. There was no point in entering into a verbal sparring match with Whitney. It wasn't the anesthesiologist's fault he himself had panicked when Moriah hadn't shown up that morning.

Sebastian needed help. Now.

Blake swallowed hard, opening and closing his fingers to relax his tense muscles. There wasn't anything else he could do for his patient but wait for Moriah's blood and finish the kid's surgery. Taking a deep breath, he once again picked up the forceps. This time, his hands remained steady.

He focused his attention on where he'd been with the original surgery, prior to the power going off. Within moments the door to the OR suite opened and the circulating nurse stepped in. "I have the second unit of O negative blood donated by Dr Howe."

"Great." Whitney took the unit from the nurse's hands and Blake watched as he proceeded to hang the unit on the IV pole. It was an odd sensation, knowing the blood was Moriah's. Whitney opened the clamp so the blood could run in freely.

Blake tore his gaze from the blood and turned his attention to the operation at hand. He cut the tendon and released the contracture.

"His pressure is climbing, up to 93 over 50. Pulse is down to 106. He's oxygenating better, almost 88 per cent—nope, now it's 90 per cent."

"All right, let's finish this surgery." Thankful his patient was doing better, Blake quickly maneuvered the tendon into place then began the painstaking task of re-attaching it. At least Sebastian wouldn't die from his error.

But he very well could have.

"I'm giving him a dose of steroids, to control any possible blood transfusion reactions from receiving un-crossmatched blood." Whitney continued to inform Blake what he was doing. Then Moriah returned to the room, using her crutches.

"How is he?" she asked in a worried tone.

"Fine, your blood helped to stabilize him. See?" Whitney handed her the patient's clipboard, displaying the pertinent information for her to read.

"I'm so glad."

Blake glanced at her. Moriah's face, the part he could see above her mask, was pale. "Are you all right? You look like you're about to faint."

She raised a brow. "I'm fine. Don't worry about me. Terrance, I'm ready to take over here. Thanks again for your help."

"No problem. He's all yours."

Blake should have been relieved everything was going better, but as he worked he couldn't erase the image of Sebastian's bright red blood pooling in the incision site. If the power had stayed out a minute or two longer—no, it didn't bear thinking about what might have happened.

There wasn't time to wallow in self-pity. He finished the surgery on Sebastian's arm, then went to the affected leg on the same side. There was still plenty of work to do before Sebastian could be transferred out of the OR suite and into the post-anesthesia recovery area.

Blake forced himself to eat something from the hospital cafeteria, although he wasn't hungry. He knew Sebastian was doing all right. He hadn't left the PACU until he was reassured the boy was stable.

Shoving his half-eaten food aside, he scrubbed his hands over his face. The accidental nicking of Sebastian's brachial artery weighed heavily on his mind. Unfortunately, it wasn't the first time in his medical career he'd made a mistake. He would never forget the case during his residency, when the patient had taken a turn for the worse during the course of surgery and Blake hadn't noticed.

Part of the blame rested with the anesthesiologist who hadn't said a word, but had continued to give higher and higher doses of medication to keep the patient stable. A good portion of the blame, though, was his. He'd forgotten the number-one rule of medicine—

always look at your patient first. He'd been so intent on the intricate details of performing surgery, he'd forgotten to step back and look at the patient as a whole.

Mistakes were never easy to deal with, and some would argue that this one with Sebastian wasn't his fault. The power had gone out at the worst possible time. Still, there was no denying his fingers had been holding the scalpel that had nicked the artery. Even if the power had gone off, he shouldn't have flinched. Holding steady was a surgeon's responsibility, no matter what area he specialized in.

Resolutely, he stood and carried his tray to the dirty-dish line. He was finished operating for the day, but he was too restless to leave the hospital. Instead he found himself returning to the PACU.

"Where's Sebastian?" he asked the PACU nurse, whose name escaped him.

"He's been transferred to his room, number 224."

"Thanks." Blake knew Sebastian must be fine, they wouldn't have transferred him if he wasn't, but he headed to the second-floor patient rooms anyway.

When he poked his head into the room, he found the seventeen-year-old boy resting comfortably. There was no sign of Sebastian's family, the ones who normally provided primary care-giving while the patient was in the hospital, so he pulled up a chair and sat down, content to watch the boy as he slept.

"Blake?"

He must have dozed because Moriah's quiet voice startled him. A glance at his watch proved he'd been sitting at Sebastian's bedside for almost an hour. Moriah stood in the doorway with a worried expression on her face.

"Yeah?"

"It's late. Come back to the hotel. You need to get some sleep." Her furrowed brow betrayed her anxiety.

She was right, but leaving Sebastian wasn't easy. The lack of family staying at his bedside concerned him. "I don't want to leave him alone."

"His mother is right here. She stayed outside here because she didn't want to wake you."

"Oh." Feeling foolish, he stood and reluctantly followed Moriah into the hall. A middle-aged woman was seated in a chair just outside the door.

The woman smiled and ducked her head shyly when he greeted her, then hurried into Sebastian's room. So much for trying to be helpful. All he'd managed had been to keep the boy's mother from visiting.

Moriah fell into step beside him as they headed down the hall, through the hospital. "Are you all right?"

"Fine." He didn't really want to talk about what had happened. His nerves were still raw, and not just from the incident with Sebastian. Every nerve in his body strained to be with Moriah.

She didn't seem to notice his internal battle. "I want to ask you about the surgery schedule. I need your help to get Henri scheduled."

"Shouldn't be a problem. His surgery won't take long, I'm sure we can squeeze him in between two previously scheduled cases." He was more than willing to do Henri's surgery whenever he could.

"Well, actually, I need you to do him on Sunday," Moriah confessed as they stepped outside. He frowned when she noticed she'd ditched her crutches. "You see, Henri told me his mother passed away a few months ago. He's been living in the orphanage. I managed to get consent from the sister in charge, who is his legal guardian, but there isn't anyone to take care of him while he's in the hospital. I'm off on Monday, so I'd like you to do his procedure tomorrow."

"Wait a minute." Blake tried to follow her convoluted logic. He stopped and turned to face her. "Henri's mother died? When did he tell you this?"

"I saw him with a group from the orphanage one day." She lifted her palms helplessly. "I'm sorry, I must have forgotten to mention it."

"Poor kid." Blake experienced a new kinship with the boy. He'd often felt like an orphan those first few years. At least he'd had his aunt and uncle to take care of him. Henri didn't have anyone.

"Not according to Sister Rita. She thinks he's the greatest thing in the world. She couldn't say enough positive things about him." Moriah arched her brow. "That's where I was earlier this morning, getting in touch with her so I could officially get her consent. So will you, please, do Henri's surgery on Sunday?"

Damn. Could this day get any worse? Moriah hadn't skipped out that morning because of some secret desire to avoid him. No, she'd been worried about Henri. The poor kid certainly deserved the chance to regain full use of his burned hand. If he'd had doubts before, he didn't now. "Yes. I'll do his surgery on Sunday."

"Thanks." Relief was evident on her features. He'd expected that, but he wasn't prepared for her to throw her arms around his neck and kiss him.

His first instinct was to lock her close, but then reality hit hard. This was exactly where he wanted her, and it was also exactly how he'd manage to hurt her. Again. When would he learn? With a quick movement he firmly pulled her arms away and stepped back.

"Ah...I have to go. See you later." Gathering all his strength, he turned and left. But, damn, it wasn't easy.

"Blake! Wait, please."

But he kept on walking, his stomach clenching tighter and tighter with every step.

Moriah stumbled over a rock on the road, wincing at the added pressure on her ankle. She'd gotten sick and tired of using the crutches so she'd tossed them aside at the end of her last case. Walking on her foot normally didn't hurt too badly but now she felt every injured muscle anew.

She swore and hauled herself upright. What was wrong with her that she allowed Blake to tear her apart like this? He couldn't have made his intent any clearer. She should be glad. Maybe now she could get on with her life, once and for all.

She sniffled and swiped at her tears. OK, so perhaps getting on with her life was impossible at the moment, seeing as they were both stuck here in Peru for the duration of the mission, but afterwards she needed to do something drastic. Pack up and move far away. She'd already left Trinity Medical Center, but maybe she needed to move to another city. Wisconsin was cold in the winter: maybe she'd head south where the temperature was warm.

Except then she'd be far away from her family.

Her anger deflated like a punctured balloon. No matter how miserable she was, the last thing she'd do was move away from her family. Her family was like a rock, always there when she needed them. In fact, she wished her sister Melanie was with her now. Melanie was one of the few who knew about her brief fling with Blake. Older by two years, Melanie had understood exactly what she'd gone through.

By the time she reached her hotel room, Moriah had wrestled her emotions under control. With a sigh, she lay on her bed and stared at the ceiling.

She was better off without Blake, she knew that. Yet watching him remain alone, sidestepping emotional entanglements, even something as basic as friendship, bothered her.

Why she cared about his apparent preference for loneliness was beyond her.

The next morning, severe stomach cramps brought Moriah out of a sound sleep. Doubled over in pain, she made her way to the bathroom in the nick of time. Why the sudden attack of nausea and diarrhea? They'd been in Peru for over a week, her body had seemingly adjusted to the food and water.

Battling painful cramps, she clutched her stomach and tried to stand. What had happened? She'd only eaten food from the hotel or the hospital cafeteria. Her mind searched back, retracing her steps the day before.

To the time she'd given blood. She remembered feeling dizzy and faint—they'd probably taken the blood too fast—but she hadn't cared, knowing Sebastian's life had depended on it. Still, when she'd nearly passed out, one of the Peruvian nurses had poured her a glass of water. She'd assumed it had been water from the hospital, but now that she thought about it, she remembered seeing the nurse with a large plastic bottle. Had the water been brought from the nurses' home? She winced. If so, it would explain why she felt so sick.

After seeming to spend hours in the bathroom, Moriah crawled back to bed. She wasn't going to make it to the hospital any time soon. She tried to grab the phone, knowing she needed to call and let someone know, but another bad cramp caught her in a vicious grip, twisting her intestines like a giant old-fashioned washing-machine wringer.

At some point someone pounded at her door, but she couldn't drag herself out of bed to answer it. In the back of her mind she hoped the person looking for her was Blake.

The pounding stopped and another wave of nausea hit hard. She barely made it to the bathroom before she was violently ill. Sweat ran in rivulets down her back, soaking her cotton nightgown so it clung to her skin.

"Moriah? Are you all right? Dammit, answer me, or I'm coming in there." Blake's warning shout echoed off the bathroom walls, reverberating against her already pounding head.

"I'm sick." The words were barely above a whisper. He flung open the bathroom door and when he saw her he immediately dropped to her side. "My God, what happened?"

"Must have drunk non-purified water after I gave blood." She should have been horribly embarrassed for Blake to find her like this, but she couldn't find the energy to care. "Can't work. Need someone to cover me."

"It's already taken care of," Blake reassured her. "Do you need help getting back to bed?"

"Please."

He stood and rinsed a washcloth in the basin, then gently wiped her face and hands, as if she were a child. The cool cloth felt heavenly and he instinctively must have known because he rinsed it out then laid it against her neck. Wrapping his arms around her, he pulled her to her feet.

There wasn't much room to maneuver in the bathroom, but he managed to get her through the doorway then lifted her in his arms and carried her to the bed.

"Sorry, can't work," she whispered.

"Shh." Blake smoothed a hand over her tangled hair. She imagined he brushed a kiss over her forehead. "Just rest, Moriah. I'll take care of everything."

She believed him. Her eyelids fluttered closed and she knew with complete certainty that Blake would indeed take care of everything.

Before collapsing into blessed sleep, she promised herself to try and talk to him later, once she felt better. Maybe he didn't realize how pushing people away only made his loneliness worse.

* * *

The room was dark when she awoke. She was instantly aware of a large male body lying on the bed beside her. In the darkness she heard Blake's slow, even breathing. He must have stayed with her all day and then fallen asleep. Sitting up, she gazed at him. His expression was peaceful and she resisted the urge to reach down to stroke his cheek. He'd been wonderful over the past few hours, taking care of her so gently and sweetly, while seeing her at her worst.

As much as she longed to linger, savoring his warmth in her bed, the pressure in her bladder urged her to get up. She gingerly pressed on her stomach with one hand. No horrific cramps: so far, so good. With a wince she swung her legs off the side of the bed and stood. Spending the day in bed had done wonders for her ankle, which hardly hurt at all any more.

Luckily the bathroom wasn't far and she made it there under her own power.

Her painful cramps were nothing more than a vivid memory. She gulped several glassfuls of water, praying they wouldn't return. Despite the early hour of four in the morning, she felt good enough to brave a shower. Ten minutes later, she felt like a new woman.

When she emerged from the bathroom, wearing nothing more than her robe, she tiptoed quietly so as not to wake Blake. But he surprised her by raising himself up on one elbow and blinking at her from across the room. "Hi."

Her lips curved in a smile and she slipped her hands into the robe pockets. He looked wonderful, warm and masculine and strong. "Hi, yourself. I'm sorry I woke you."

"I'm not. You look much better." His sleepy grin, tousled hair and bare chest transported her to the last time they'd shared a hotel room here in Peru. The intimacy of being here with him knocked her off balance. She was surprised at how much she wanted to crawl back into bed beside him. To lose herself in his arms, in the warm, musky male scent of him. She took a hesitant step forward and his smile faded. He sat up, as if to jump out of bed. "I should go."

"Don't." She held out a hand, as if by willpower alone she could make him stay. "Please, don't leave."

A strangled sound slipped from the back of his throat. "I have to go. I don't want to hurt you, like I did last time."

The tiny flare of hope withered and died, but then she didn't care. Maybe being in Peru, so far away from home, helped give her the impetus to throw caution to the wind. She still cared about Blake, despite everything that had passed between them. Maybe she was being foolish, but suddenly the one man she wanted was right in front of her and she was damned if she was going to let him go.

Her hands came up to the belt of her robe. Blake froze, staring at her as she slowly untied the belt and let the edges of the robe fall open. "You won't hurt me, I promise."

CHAPTER NINE

"HOLD it. Please, wait." Wildly, Blake tried to think of something to stop Moriah. He was just as worried about hurting her as he was about getting hurt himself. "What about…? Ah—you said you'd moved on with your life. Aren't you seeing someone?" He imagined at least a dozen guys had asked her out since their night together.

"Not at the moment." She let the edges of her robe fall open, revealing a tantalizing glimpse of bare, golden skin.

"But…" How could that be? Desperately, he tried to sound convincing as she came closer still. "Stop this. You have no idea what you're doing to me." Blake could have sworn his limbs were coated with icy slush, and his muscles refused to obey his commands. His early morning arousal didn't help him as far as doing the right thing went, especially when he was surrounded by the shower-clean scent of her.

"Oh, I think I have an idea or two." She deliberately ran her fingers through her long damp hair. "I want you, Blake. I don't think I'm far off the mark in saying you want me, too."

He bit back a harsh groan. He had to get out of here—now. Before it was too late.

He didn't move.

It was already too late.

"Moriah." All he could say was her name. It sounded like a plea.

"Yes?" She reached the edge of the bed, within arm's reach. The sultry expression in her eyes was his undoing. He wore only his boxers. The small article of clothing was too much.

Her hands reached out to stroke his chest. He sucked in a harsh breath. He wasn't strong enough to push her away.

"Come here." One tug and she tumbled into his arms. He leaned down and caught her mouth in a deep kiss.

It was too easy to convince himself he wouldn't hurt her again. She knew him now, knew his views on having a family. So since he couldn't stop kissing her long enough to formulate a coherent thought, he gave in to his need.

His fingers tangled in the robe as he pushed the bulky fabric aside. He ached to feel her silky skin against him.

"Blake." She gasped his name, as he tossed the garment into a heap on the floor. Gently, he swung her into the bed beneath him, so he could look down at her.

"Are you sure?" The light shining through the bathroom behind her cast her facial features into shadow and he hesitated, unsure if she was asking him to stay or to stop.

"I need you." She urged him close, and he nearly groaned again, reveling in the way her breasts brushed against his chest. "Please, don't leave."

"I won't." At least not now, he silently amended. Eventually, he'd have to leave her, but not at this moment. He nuzzled her neck.

Then hesitated. There was one tiny problem. Slowly he lifted his head, looking her directly in the eye. "Moriah, we can't do this. I didn't come here with protection."

Lifting her head, she pressed a hot kiss against his chest, seeming to delight in tasting him. Looping her hands around his neck, she smiled. "Check the pocket of my robe."

Lord, she'd thought of everything. He kissed her again, slowly, deeply, drawing strength from the pleasure. On one level he could have spent what was left of the night simply kissing her.

But she squirmed beneath him, silently asking for more. He raised his head, reached over the side of the bed, and groped for the robe.

"Got it." He pulled out the foil pack, but her fingers were already busily taking it from him.

She sheathed him and he nearly lost control right then and there. Not that she'd believe he hadn't been intimate with a woman since her. He clenched his jaw and reached for her hands, pulling them away and using his mouth to explore her instead.

He'd never forgotten her. Never would.

Losing himself in her womanly scent, he exchanged caress for caress, kiss for kiss, until they were both panting, writhing with need. He explored her hidden depths with his fingers, nearly whimpering when he found her slick and wet. Teasing her tiny bud, he urged her higher until he felt her clenching tremors, then thrust deep. Home. Miles away, in the desert of Peru, he'd finally found the true meaning of coming home.

But the hot urgency of his body wouldn't let him wallow in the stunning realization. Instead, he began to move, pulling back then thrusting deep. Her inner muscles tightened around him, clutching him close. Sweet Lord, pleasure spiked and he didn't know how long he'd be able to last. Not nearly as long as he'd have liked, as his groin tightened then surged with need. He eagerly followed her up and over the pinnacle of mind-blowing satisfaction.

Moriah lay still, her chest rising and falling in agitation and every nerve ending tingling with aftershocks of sensation. Blake's warmth rested heavily along her side, his arm draped across her stomach, and her lips curved in a drowsy smile. Ah, yes. This was what she'd wanted from the first moment she'd realized he'd spent the night in her bed.

His arm shifted and he lightly slid his fingers up along her side. She shivered, over-sensitized nerves rippling in reaction to his touch.

"I need you." His guttural voice rumbled near her ear.

"I think you've already had me." She tried for a light, playful tone, but when his hand cupped her breast, she gasped and instinctively arched against him, eager for more.

"I'll always need you." He pressed a trail of kisses along the curve of her jaw even as his lean surgeon's fingers plucked and played with her turgid nipple. "Always."

She tried not to read too much into his words, but then his flesh stirred and hardened against her hip. He continued his dual assault, his mouth licking and sucking along her neck, his fingers stroking her breast. He moved, just enough to spread her thighs with one knee so he could enter her from behind.

Surrounded in sensation, she eagerly opened, reveling in his sensual caress. He pulled her boneless body over until she was lying directly on top of him, one hand holding her breast, the other covering her mound as he rocked into her over and over again. With a cry, she bucked and shuddered against him in a fierce release.

Some indeterminate amount of time later she pried one eye open and peered at the clock. So far, so good: he hadn't found a way to sneak out of her bed yet. "Don't you need to make rounds?"

"Nope." He sleepily played with a lock of her hair, nuzzling her cheek. "George is covering for me. At least until the first case starts at seven-thirty."

"Hmm." She closed her eyes and burrowed against him. "Well, it's eight now."

"What?" He bolted upright, nearly spilling her to the floor. "Cripes, how did that happen? I have to get to the hospital."

"Omph." Sprawled on the bed beside him, she frowned and rubbed the spot on her head where he'd bumped her.

"I'm sorry." He planted a quick kiss on the sore spot on her head, then another on her cheek, then on her mouth for a long, deep moment, before shooting out of bed. "But I really do have to go."

"I know." Inwardly glowing from his kiss, she watched his taut backside disappear into the bathroom. She understood he had patients waiting for him and took it as a good sign that he hadn't left after the first time they'd made love.

She needed to go to the hospital as well, but would wait for her turn in the bathroom. After they'd switched places, though, she emerged from the bathroom only to find he was gone.

The hollow feeling in her stomach reinforced what her brain was already telling her. Blake was still Blake.

They'd spent another incredible night together. But, like last time, nothing had really changed.

On her way to the hospital, she remembered she needed to drive out to the orphanage to pick up Henri. Since his surgery was scheduled for the next day, she'd have to find a way to get him either tonight or tomorrow morning.

She'd have to remember to ask Blake about the taxi service, and tried to remember how far it was to the orphanage.

It had been days since she'd seen Henri and she wondered how he was doing. She missed seeing him hang around, as he'd done last year.

Of course, that had been before his mother had passed away.

Sister Rita made it sound as if Henri had fit right in at the orphanage, though, so she probably didn't need to worry about him.

Moriah discovered Terrance was the anesthesiologist in Blake's room, working on a patient with a cleft lip and palate. When she reviewed the file, she discovered their patient was a five-year-old girl, one who'd suffered multiple sinus infections as a result of the split in her palate.

"Blood pressure stable, 92 over 45 with a pulse of 118 and a pulse ox of 98 per cent." Terrance recited the vitals for Blake's benefit.

Moriah smiled to herself. Obviously Terrance had figured out how to keep Blake happy. Nudging Terrance with her elbow, she gestured for him to move aside. "I can take over now. Thanks for covering my patients."

"How are you feeling?" Terrance stood, but gave her an intent look over the top of his face mask. "You still look a little pale, although I see you're not using the crutches any more."

"Nope, my ankle is much better and so am I." She assumed his vacated seat. "Did you have to cover all my surgeries yesterday, too?"

"Yeah, but, hey, I told you there would be payback time," he joked.

"Yeah, yeah. Promises, promises." She wasn't too worried, they didn't have many days off to play with. "How did things go? Any problems?"

"Nah, everything went fine. We're still on schedule, we didn't postpone any patients."

"Thank heavens for that. I would have felt horrible if we'd had to cancel cases. Did we add any others to the list?"

"Besides Henri, you mean?" Terrance shook his head. "Not yet, although I think George is seeing a few additional potential candidates today, between patients."

The same thing had happened last year: more patients continuing to arrive, long after they'd put their schedule together. If the required surgery wasn't too time-consuming, they might be able to make room. Anything to avoid turning patients away.

Thankfully, Blake's first case of the day went without a hitch. An hour and a half later, Moriah wheeled little Arianna into the PACU.

"Greta, I have another patient for you," Moriah called, interrupting the nurse's quiet conversation with Terrance.

"Coming." Greta hurried over. "Oh, isn't she a cutie? Blake did a great job on her."

"She sailed through the surgery but, considering her history of sinus infections, we'll need to cover her with antibiotics."

"Of course." Greta took over Arianna's care. "I'll take care of it."

"Call me if you need anything." For a moment she hesitated, loath to leave as she remembered Louisa who'd woken up thrashing like a wild woman, but that had been due to a non-functioning IV. In contrast, Arianna seemed fine.

"I will." Greta's gaze softened as she dug in her pack for a stuffed animal for the girl.

The day went on. They managed to get two more patients finished before the last one arrived. From her first look at him, Moriah knew this would be a long one. The poor guy had obviously sustained severe facial burns. Blake would do a split-thickness skin graft to replace some of the debilitated scar tissue.

Moriah was thankful the patient was otherwise fairly healthy, because his surgery did indeed take several hours. She was amazed at how painstakingly Blake worked, never losing his patience or complaining. When he glanced up at her, his expression was full of concern.

"Should I reverse him?" Moriah asked.

"Not yet. I don't like the look of this." Blake stared down at the area in question. "Keep him intubated for now. He may need more surgery if this flap goes bad."

She gave the patient several breaths with the ambubag, as Blake steadily watched the graft. Every few minutes he'd test the flap to see if it would blanch with pressure and how long it took for the pink color to return. He also poked it with a needle to see if it would bleed.

"What I wouldn't give for a few leeches," he muttered.

"I'm sure they have leeches in Peru," she responded dryly. "Although I doubt they're sterile." Back in the States, they sometimes needed to use leeches to help get rid of the excess blood pooling underneath a skin flap. As barbaric as it sounded, the therapy was amazingly successful. The leeches, bred in sterile conditions specifically for this purpose, instinctively stayed on the flap, removing the worst of the blood accumulation underneath and preventing further surgeries.

"The threat of infection might be worth it, to avoid further surgery," Blake commented.

She knew he was right. "Should we send someone to the river to find some?" Ick, she thought with a shiver. Anyone but her, that was.

Blake hesitated. "Let's hold off for now. He seems to be doing all right. Go ahead and reverse him."

Moriah reversed the anesthesia and after a few minutes she removed the breathing tube and wheeled him into the PACU.

"I can't believe it's so late," she murmured. Now that surgical list was over, she was aware of her stiff and sore muscles, partly from having been so sick the day before.

Greta smiled. "I must admit, I'm glad this is the last patient."

"Me, too." Moriah watched as the nurse administered a little oxygen.

Blake arrived from the OR suites. "How's the skin flap?"

Moriah pressed a finger lightly against his handiwork. "About the same. A little pale, but still blanching."

"Blanching slower, I think." Blake frowned. "That's OK, I'll stick around for a while, strip the drains to encourage the blood to drain while I keep an eye on it."

"I understand." She tried to hide her dismay. He could be using this case as an excuse to avoid her, although she knew he really cared about his patient. The

Peruvian nurses on the general wards weren't trained to do flap checks every fifteen minutes, like they were in the States. She suspected that even if they were trained, Blake would still want to stick around to check his work. "Do you want me to stay with you?"

"No, there's no need for both of us to stay." Blake settled in beside his patient, barely sparing her a glance. "You were sick, you need to rest."

"So do you." She watched him, trying to read his mind. Did he already regret their intimacy? Was he right now trying to think of a way to let her down gently? Well, he needn't bother. She hadn't been lying when she'd told him he wouldn't hurt her.

Well, maybe she was a little hurt. But at least this time she'd gone to bed with him already knowing there wouldn't be a long-term relationship between them.

"I'm fine. Don't worry about me."

Peachy. Now they were both fine. She understood what he was really telling her. "All right, I won't. Goodnight, Blake."

"Goodnight, Moriah."

She could feel the weight of his gaze on her back as she left the PACU. Had he expected heated protests? Theatrics? Or, worse, tears? Hesitating in the doorway, she drummed up the nerve to glance back at him.

He was bent over his patient, concentrating intensely on the skin flap.

She turned back, hardening her resolve. Not this time. She wasn't that foolish.

CHAPTER TEN

MORIAH didn't sleep very well. Blake's scent clung to her pillow and sheets, filling her head until she ached with wanting. She rose early, having arranged for a taxi to take her over to the orphanage first thing that morning.

Blake caught her in the hotel lobby as she was about to head outside. "Where are you going?"

"To pick up Henri."

Blake didn't seem nearly as exhausted as she'd expected after staying up most of the night. "I'll come with you."

Surprised by his offer, she shrugged. "Fine with me, although wouldn't you rather get some sleep?"

"I managed to get about five hours' worth," Blake admitted, following her outside into the bright sunlight. A tall, lean man waited patiently beside the taxi. "Hey, you hired the same guy."

"I know." Moriah smiled at the driver. "Bernardo, it's nice to see you again."

"*Señorita*." He nodded at her, then politely opened the door for them.

Once they were settled inside, there was a lengthy

awkward silence. Just when she was figuring it would be a very long drive, Blake turned toward her. "I bet you think I should have known the guy's name."

Yes, she did, but she tried to choose her words carefully. "You know, Blake, it's obvious you care very much for your patients, but outside of work, you hold yourself aloof. I understand why, I realize your childhood was painful, but the good thing about being an adult is the ability to make choices. Choosing to loosen up a little, to talk to people more, might be a place to start."

He didn't take offense at her suggestion, but actually seemed to be seriously considering her words. "I guess I could try."

"So how is your flap patient doing—what was his name?" She knew very well what the patient's name was, but he didn't need to know that.

"José, and he's doing fine. Luckily, the flap took. But I spent a good couple of hours doing fifteen-minute flap checks to be sure. I fell asleep in the doctors' lounge about one-thirty this morning."

"I'm glad." How interesting Blake could open up to his patients and their families, but never bother to ask the taxi driver's name. Maybe he didn't realize how he perpetuated his loneliness after all.

She tried to ignore the tiny flare of hope, telling herself this revelation didn't mean anything.

He closed his eyes and she fell silent, knowing how much he needed to sleep. But ten minutes later he reached over to take her hand in his. "I missed you last night."

Her pulse kicked upward when his warm, strong fingers wrapped protectively around hers. She couldn't help but smile. "What was that, a power nap?"

"Yeah. Works wonders."

She laughed, then added, "I missed you, too."

Holding her gaze, he picked up her hand and pressed a kiss on the back. She melted a little at the gallant gesture.

"So how far is it to the orphanage?" He surreptitiously tugged her closer.

"I don't have the faintest idea," she murmured, unable to resist his unspoken request. She leaned closer, craving his embrace.

His gaze remained solemn when he looked at her. "Have I mentioned how beautiful you are?"

She caught her breath. "No."

"I should have." He lowered his head and she eagerly met him more than halfway.

She enjoyed his kiss for a long moment, then pulled back, looking into his eyes. "What's going on, between us, Blake?"

He shrugged and brushed a stray curl from her cheek. "I don't know. I'm not making promises about the future, but I can't seem to get you out of my blood. My life hasn't been the same since I left you last year. I don't know what it means but, I swear, I'm not playing games with you."

For some reason, she believed him. When she leaned forward to kiss him again, the taxi stopped.

"*Señorita*, we have arrived," Bernardo announced in Spanish from the front seat.

With a groan, Blake lifted his head. "Great timing, Bernardo," he muttered in a sour tone.

Moriah giggled but refrained from pointing out Blake's power nap had wasted a good portion of their time. Still, she almost wished she'd instructed Bernardo to take the scenic route. Regretfully, she moved away and got out of the taxi. "I'll just be a minute."

She hurried to the front door of the orphanage and knocked. Henri opened the door. *"La médica!"*

"Hola, Henri." Behind the boy she saw the wide girth of Sister Rita. "Hello, Sister."

"Won't you come in?" the woman asked. "I promised you a tour."

"I'd love a tour, but we're pressed for time." Moriah gave her an apologetic glance. "Would you mind waiting until I bring Henri back after his surgery?"

"Of course not. Thanks for coming out to pick him up." The woman truly seemed to have the personality of a saint, as nothing bothered her in the least. "Take care, now. I'll see you soon."

Moriah clasped Henri's hand in hers as they headed back toward the taxi. The boy climbed in, settling between the two adults.

Blake cleared his throat. "So, Henri. How are you?"

"Bueno." The boy grinned from ear to ear. "I didn't have to study today."

Just like every other kid in the world, Henri didn't seem to mind being forced to miss school. "Hmm. Guess you'll have to study harder to make up the lost time, won't you?" Moriah pointed out.

Henri nodded. "It's OK, I like to study. Most of the

time." He lifted up his deformed hand. "But I also want to learn how to make things with my hands, so I'm happy to have this be the day for my surgery."

Blake's troubled gaze rested on Henri, and Moriah wondered what he was thinking.

"I'm glad I can help your hand so you can make things, Henri." Blake paused, then added, "But if you could be anything you wanted, in the whole world, what would you do?"

"That's easy." Henri pointed at both of them. "I would become a doctor, so I could help all the children who have been burned by fire. Just like you."

Moriah lightly brushed her hand over his head, overcome with emotion. "That's an admirable wish, Henri," she said when she could speak.

Blake simply nodded, but this time his gaze lingered on Henri, and she suspected he was seeing himself in the boy's earnest eyes.

Henri continued to chatter as Bernardo pulled up in front of the hotel. When she would have paid the fare, Blake insisted on paying it himself. As they walked down the street to the hospital, a strangely familiar car rushed past them, coming to a jarring stop in front of the emergency entrance.

"Manuel?" Moriah recognized the young man who shot from the car almost before it stopped. He immediately rounded the car to open the passenger door and she caught a glimpse of Rasha inside. She quickened her pace. "Oh, God, something's wrong with the baby."

"What baby?" Blake asked, then he remembered

her mentioning she'd helped a woman deliver her baby on their first day.

Moriah didn't answer, her attention centered on the woman emerging from her car. "Rasha, what happened?"

Tears streamed down her cheeks as she held her crying baby. Even to Blake's inexpert ears, the crying didn't seem normal. "She spit up, then choked. I tried to get the stuff out of her mouth, but she turned blue."

Moriah quickly took over, turning the infant on her belly and using her index finger to help hold the mouth open. "It's all right, everything is going to be just fine."

"Let's get the baby inside." Blake belatedly opened the emergency-department doors and ushered them inside. Infants were out of his league, unless they needed something surgically repaired. Helplessly, he watched as Moriah took the baby into a room and immediately began to assess it.

He ran his hand through his hair, unable to remember if the baby was a boy or a girl.

Using a suction ball, provided by one of the nurses, Moriah suctioned out the baby's nose and mouth. "Her pulse is high—210—and her respirations are fast, too. But her pulse ox seems to be a little better, up to 90 per cent."

A girl. Blake could barely see much of the baby, with the adults gathered around, but he heard what Moriah said.

The baby was a girl.

He didn't know why he felt compelled to know the sex of the child. He felt useless as he watched. Rasha and Manuel were certainly concerned parents. With every look, every gesture they showed their love for their baby. Clearly, they were the perfect family. The sounds of the baby's crying changed to smaller, hiccuping sobs, without the hoarseness of earlier.

"There, she's doing better already, see?" Moriah cradled the baby in her arms. "Her pulse and respirations are returning to normal."

"She'll need some antibiotics to ward off pneumonia." He finally found his voice. The image of Moriah holding a baby sent a shock wave vibrating through him. For someone who didn't want children, he could all too easily see his baby in her arms.

Except he didn't particularly like kids.

Actually, it wasn't as if he disliked them. He just couldn't understand why people willingly took on such an overwhelmingly serious responsibility. A *lifelong* responsibility.

"I agree." Moriah met his gaze, then frowned. "Is that you being paged?"

"Huh?" He hadn't heard a thing.

One of the Peruvian nurses entered the room. "Dr Powers? There is a request for you to go to the OR."

"Thanks for letting me know." He met Moriah's gaze. "I'll see you later."

"I'll be up soon," she promised.

He'd nearly forgotten Henri until he saw him hovering in the doorway. "Henri, I'll see you later, too, when it's time to do surgery on your hand."

Henri nodded. "You saved the baby."

Wryly, Blake shook his head. "Not me. Moriah did all the work."

"Thank you." Manuel stepped forward, taking Blake's hand and pumping it enthusiastically. "For coming when you did."

Blake nodded, refraining from stating the obvious again. He slipped out of the cubicle and strode through the emergency department to the elevators that would take him to the first-floor operating rooms. His views on life seemed confused and he didn't like it one bit.

He especially hadn't liked feeling helpless during the mini-crisis. Performing plastic surgery on small children was one thing, saving their lives was altogether different.

George waited for him in the main OR. "Sorry to bother you, but I have another sick surgeon. If you can, I need you to operate."

"No problem. I planned on doing Henri's surgery later anyway."

"Thanks. Your patient is in room three." George hurried off.

Blake quickly changed out of his street clothes into scrubs. As he began to wash his hands in the large sink, he thought about Moriah. He'd followed her into the cab this morning on impulse. Holding hands with her, kissing her, hadn't been nearly enough.

He longed for more.

Last night, he'd have given anything to follow her back to her room. Maybe tonight?

Wait a minute. He pulled himself up short. What was he thinking? If he continued to spend time with her on this trip, leaving her would be twice as hard. For both of them.

Seeing Moriah with Rasha's baby had only reinforced what he already knew. Moriah was looking for
a long-term relationship. Right after Ryan had pro-
posed she'd confided that one of her reasons for becoming an anesthesiologist had been because once she
had children, it would be easier to work part-time
hours.

Children, plural. Meaning she was planning a large
family, just like her own.

Remembering Moriah's loud, boisterous family,
where no one seemed to pay attention to anyone else,
he almost winced. He knew that wasn't what he
wanted. His life with his aunt and uncle hadn't been
horrible; in fact, things had often been quiet and peaceful.

Until they'd died, first his uncle from a massive stroke
then his aunt a year later. She'd seemed to wither away
until she'd joined her husband, leaving Blake alone again.

Pushing away his thoughts, he finished scrubbing
and headed into OR suite three. Luckily, the patient was
a simple contracture release, very similar to one he'd
done the other day. He reviewed the record for a few
minutes, then began to operate.

And wondered when Moriah would be joining him.

Hours later, he still hadn't seen Moriah, and had no
idea where she was until he entered the OR where
Henri's case was scheduled.

There she was, talking to Henri and trying to put the
boy at ease.

"I promise, I'll be here when you wake up," she told
him, as she gently infused some medication into his IV.

Henri nodded and closed his eyes. Blake watched as Moriah gathered the equipment she'd need to place his breathing tube.

"I wondered where you were," he commented as he began to arrange the surgical trays the way he liked them.

"George needed assistance, so I worked in his room then went to see Henri. I think he was more nervous than he let on."

He didn't blame the boy for being nervous. "Are you sure you're up for this?" he asked with a frown. "There's bound to be another anesthesiologist who wouldn't mind doing Henri's case for you."

She shot him a startled look. "Why? I'm fine. Really, he's just another patient."

Blake highly doubted Henri was just a patient. Moriah seemed to have a more intense interest in Henri than in any of the other kids. Even if she wasn't ready to admit it herself, Henri was different.

Heck, he wasn't so sure he could blithely operate on the boy either. Henri's cheeky grin flashed in his mind's eye. What if something horrible happened during the procedure? His gut clenched and he took a calming breath.

With an effort he cleared his mind. He wasn't attached to the boy, not like Moriah was. She was a natural with kids.

The thought troubled him. Because the thought of Moriah bearing another man's child was painful.

Worse than that, the very image made him feel slightly sick.

He shook off the depressing notion. There wasn't time for this. He had surgery to perform. One thing was for sure, he knew Moriah well enough to know she was a professional. If she were overly emotionally involved in Henri's care, she'd step aside and assign someone else to take over. Just as he would in the same situation.

"All right, let me know when you're ready," Blake instructed.

"Just about." She'd already placed Henri's breathing tube and was in the process of connecting him to the anesthesia machine. "There. Just let me give the first dose of antibiotics, then you can get started."

"Sounds good." He'd thought working with her after the night they'd shared would be difficult but, in fact, he was glad she was there. He liked hearing the sound of her voice as she took care of the patients, appreciated having her at his side during a crisis. Like the power outage the other day. There was no one calmer in an emergency than Moriah. He gently examined Henri's burned fingers, deciding how best to tackle the problem of releasing the contractures.

"Ready to go," Moriah announced.

"Great." He decided to work on the middle finger first, since that was the digit crucial to gaining more movement in the rest of his hand.

He made his first incision, and was just preparing to detach the tendon when Moriah cried out, "Blake! Henri's covered with hives. He must be allergic to the antibiotic."

Blake glanced up. "Get a dose of epinephrine ready."

"I already gave some Benadryl and one milligram of epinephrine." Moriah's voice was uncharacteristically shaky. "There's no record of penicillin allergies in his chart. Didn't we use penicillin last time we operated on him?"

"Actually, I don't think we did. We used Cefoxin last time." A fact he only knew because he'd read the boy's chart to review what he'd planned to do. He glanced at Moriah, trying to read her eyes. "Should we abort the procedure? We can always make room for him in another couple of days."

"No, I think the epinephrine is working." She appeared calmer now. "The hives are still there, but they aren't getting any worse. And he's already intubated and oxygenating fine, luckily."

"I'll continue to operate, if that's what you want." Blake heard the underlying tremor in her voice and knew this decision had to be hers alone. She was the one closest to the boy. "Your choice, Moriah."

"Go ahead, he's doing fine." Her dark gaze met his. "I'd rather get this over with, if you don't mind."

"All right, then." Blake turned his attention back to Henri's hand. "Hopefully this won't take long."

He worked over the small fingers in Henri's hand, cutting the scar tissue so the fingers could be used again. He only needed to do a few small grafts to help repair the damaged tendons.

After an hour and a half he stepped back and stretched his aching muscles. "All finished. I think he'll actually have more use of the damaged fingers than I'd originally anticipated."

"Do you want me to reverse him?" Moriah asked.

"Go ahead." Blake pulled off his bloody gloves. "He's all yours."

"Gee, thanks." Moriah removed the breathing tube and then covered Henri's mouth and nose with an oxygen mask. "I'll take him over to the PACU."

"I'll catch up with you in a few minutes. I want to take a quick peek at José's skin flap." Blake watched Moriah push Henri on the gurney out of the OR suite to head down the hall to the PACU. He was just as glad to have that particular procedure over with, too. After pulling off his bloody hospital gown, he crossed over to the sink. He spent a few minutes washing up, then headed out of the OR to the patient rooms.

José was on the second floor and when he entered the room he spoke softly so as not to startle the patient. "José? It's me, Dr Powers. I need to check your flap again. I'm going to flick on the big lights, OK?"

José nodded and Blake turned on the bright overhead lights. He bent down and examined the flap. Thank heavens, it was doing well. He'd been so worried last night, thinking he'd have to return to surgery to relieve the build-up of blood beneath the flap.

"Looks great." He grinned down at José. "Have you seen how it looks in the mirror?" When José shook his head, Blake went out to the nurses' station to find a mirror. He brought it in and held it up to show him. "See? The scarred area is covered now and you can turn your head from side to side."

"Gracias, el médico. Muchas gracias." José gave him a lopsided smile.

"You're welcome. I'll check with you in the morning." Blake returned the mirror to the nurses' station. Once he was on the floor, he figured he should check on his other patients as well.

So he finished his rounds, then glanced at his watch. Surely Moriah would be finished with Henri by now.

He walked back toward the recovery room, in time to see a nurse named Emily shut off the lights and close the door. "Wait a minute, where's Henri? And Dr Howe?"

"Dr Howe took Henri to his room." Emily seemed surprised by his question. "He was our last patient."

"Do you know which room?" he asked.

"Third floor, 314, I believe."

Blake retraced his steps to the elevators and this time headed to the third floor. He found room 314 without any trouble, since the layout was exactly the same as on the second floor.

The room was dark, only a crack of light could be seen from beneath the bathroom door. He gave his eyes a moment to adjust to the darkness, then frowned when he saw Moriah curled up in a chair next to Henri's bed, her head as close to his as possible.

For a moment he didn't understand, until it clicked. Of course, she'd planned on staying with the child throughout the night.

She looked so peaceful. Seeing her with Henri made him feel strangely bereft. Last night he hadn't been able to go back to the hotel with her because his patient had needed him; now she was stuck here with Henri. Then he smiled. Actually, with her native American heritage, she could easily be mistaken for Henri's mother.

His smile faded. There was that mother image again. He could picture it so clearly, her belly round with child, a little boy or girl, with olive skin and lots of dark hair like hers.

She'd mentioned having choices. Obviously, he had two different ones now. He could walk away, giving her the chance to find someone else, someone who'd give her the family she wanted.

Or he could keep moving forward, giving their relationship a chance to grow.

But was it fair to ask Moriah put her dreams of having a family on hold—permanently?

CHAPTER ELEVEN

MORIAH stirred when Henri thrashed in his sleep. She raised her head and glanced down at him. He was another star patient, never once asking for a drop of pain medicine. She knew his fingers had to hurt, but every time she'd asked, he'd denied being in pain.

Still, she'd kept a few doses of morphine for him and had even gone as far as to give him some against his will. At least the medication had helped him sleep for almost six hours. Since then, though, he'd refused any more.

The longer she spent time with him, the more he reminded her of her nephew Mitch. The identical look of disdain when she'd tried to convince him to finish all his food prior to eating dessert. The way he slept, with the utter relaxation of the innocent. Heck, she could imagine the boys playing together, having a great time despite their cultural differences. Henri's English was surprisingly good.

With a yawn she stood and stretched her aching muscles. Sleeping in the chair had given her a few more kinks to work out. At least her ankle was nearly back to normal. It didn't hurt at all, unless she twisted it a certain way.

Borrowing Henri's bathroom, she washed up and tried to finger-comb her hair. The hour was still early, but she knew Blake would make rounds soon.

When he arrived, she greeted him with a wide smile, but her stomach sank when he remained totally professional, asking her questions about Henri's care as if she really were only a patient's family member instead of the woman he'd taken to bed and made love to.

She narrowed her gaze in annoyance. He was doing it again, distancing himself from her. She knew it, yet she was helpless to stop it.

"How is Henri doing?"

"Great. He only took one dose of morphine, though. He's refused to take any more," Moriah told him.

"Hmm. Well, as long as the pain doesn't interfere with his sleep, he'll be fine." Blake kept his gaze trained on the chart. "I'm glad to see his rash has abated."

"Me, too." Moriah frowned. This was ridiculous. Hadn't they gotten past this? He hadn't acted like this in the taxi yesterday. He'd kissed her hand then pulled her closer for a proper kiss. What was wrong with him? "I thought I'd check in with George to see if he needs any help, since Henri's doing so well. I don't think Henri will need constant care all day. I can help cover lunches and breaks as needed."

"I'm sure George will appreciate the help." When Blake finally met her gaze, his was impersonally remote. "I'll need you to change the dressing on Henri's fingers at seven o'clock tonight."

"I will." Perplexed, she watched him walk away. What on earth had changed? Clearly, something must be bothering him. But she was darned if she could decipher what it was. She hadn't done anything, except take care of Henri.

Moriah decided she'd corner Blake later and pressure him into telling her what was wrong. But for now she focused her attention on her patient.

Henri reassured her he was fine, urging her to leave him alone for a while. After promising him she'd return later, she headed down to the first-floor operating suites.

She met George leaving as she was on her way in. "Moriah!" he greeted her. "Do you have a minute?"

"Sure. In fact, I was just coming down to offer my services. What's up?"

"One of the locals called to let me know there's another potential patient asking to be seen. I'd like you to come and examine her with me." George turned and led the way to the clinic. "She's a sixteen-year-old girl, and may feel more comfortable with a female physician."

"No problem." Moriah hurried to keep up with him. "Any idea what sort of surgery she needs?"

"Nope." George opened the door for her and gestured for her to go through. "But we'll find out soon enough. She's waiting for us in room ten."

Moriah opened the door to clinic room ten, to see a young girl holding a hand over her mouth, seated next to an older man. The man stood the moment they entered.

"Hello." He spoke slowly in Spanish. "My name is Theo and this is my daughter, Marita. We have walked for the past six days, from dawn to sundown, to come here. We'd like to ask if you could please fix Marita's face."

Moriah's jaw dropped. Good grief, the two of them had actually walked for six whole days just to get here? Talk about persistence. She summoned a smile for the girl. "Hello, Marita. What seems to be the problem?" She reached up to draw the girl's hand from her face, but the girl resisted, shaking and ducking her head.

"I'm sorry, Marita is shy about you seeing it." Theo's brow furrowed. "Marita has had this defect since birth. But she is growing worse now that she is older. She has refused to leave the house, not wanting anyone to see her." He sent them a beseeching look. "Please, help her. Marita is very depressed. Two months ago she tried to take her own life."

This was serious. Moriah stepped forward, speaking slowly to Marita. "I'm a doctor, Marita. Please, let me see your mouth. Dr Litmann here is a surgeon, it's possible he can help you."

Marita closed her eyes and dropped her hand, revealing one of the most grotesque cases of cleft lip Moriah had ever seen. Of course, most cases didn't go untreated for as long as Marita's had. George took one look at her and sighed. "There's no way we can leave her like this. I know the schedule is full but we'll find a way to fit her in."

"*Gracias.*" Theo smiled in relief and wrapped his arm around his daughter's shoulders. "We are so grateful. *Gracias.*"

Moriah glanced at George. "Today is my day off, but if you can find a surgeon, I'll do the anesthesia for her procedure."

"Great. Thanks, Moriah." George hurried off while Moriah finished examining Marita. Thankfully, the girl was in fairly good health, if you didn't count severe depression.

"Have you eaten anything today?" she asked. When Marita hesitated and glanced at her father, Moriah added, "It's important for me to know if there is food in your stomach. If you have eaten, I just need to know when. Either way, you will still have surgery, I promise."

Marita's hand was back over her mouth and it was several long seconds before she slowly shook her head.

"When we left home six days ago, we had some food, but it's all gone now. We have not eaten since yesterday," Theo finally explained.

Oh, Lord. Moriah's throat thickened with emotion. How completely amazing that they'd walked six days for the possibility of surgery. Would any American do something like that? She couldn't imagine it. Taking a slow, deep breath, she forced a smile. "Well, that's good news for you, Marita. Now we can operate on your lip sooner." She glanced at the girl's father. "I think you must be hungry. After I get Marita settled in, we'll find something for you."

"Don't worry about me. Take care of my daughter."

His concern for his daughter was sweet. Theo was obviously a great father.

George returned with Blake. He barely spared her a

glance, but instantly smiled warmly at their shy patient. "Hello, Marita. My name is Dr Powers. Dr Litmann was telling me about your need for surgery. May I see?"

Once again Marita resisted, until her father convinced her to co-operate. She closed her eyes and dropped her hand, as if she could only bear for them to look if she couldn't see them. Blake immediately turned to George. "I'm more than willing to do her surgery, if we have an open room."

"OR suite four is occupied until three o'clock this afternoon, then it's free. I've already made arrangements to use the room then."

"Great." Blake nodded. "I'll plan on it."

She didn't have any time to discuss what was bothering Blake, because once they'd gotten Marita and her father settled into a patient room, she ended up returning to the OR to cover another anesthesiologist for a break. By the time she was finished, it was time to go back and check on Henri, then start covering for lunches.

Moriah remained busy up until three o'clock when she was scheduled to do Marita's case with Blake. As she spoke to the girl, explaining what she was going to do, she was aware of Blake entering the room. She concentrated on placing Marita's IV, then gave her a small dose of sedative to help her relax.

"I'll have her ready to go in a few minutes," Moriah called out to Blake. "Just let me get her intubated."

"No problem." Blake didn't seem annoyed with the minor delay and Moriah wondered if she'd imagined his cool response earlier. Maybe she had been imagining things. They were both exhausted from the long hours they were keeping. They'd gotten close in the taxi, maybe all they needed was a little downtime together. She quickly placed Marita's breathing tube, using the girl's nasal passage so Blake could repair her lip, then connected her to the anesthesia machine.

"I'm all set here." Moriah quickly jotted down Marita's initial set of vital signs.

One of the scrub nurses came over to place sterile drapes over Marita's head and chest, leaving an open area where only her mouth could be seen. Once the area was prepped, Blake approached. Because of the site of the surgery and her position at the head of the bed, they would have to work in close physical proximity.

Blake didn't seem to be holding back from her as they worked over Marita. They immediately fell into the same rhythm they'd had before Blake had started acting so strangely. Thankfully, the repair of the cleft lip didn't take very long, although just as Blake was finishing, the anesthesia machine indicated the gas tank was empty, when she knew there should be a good half-tank left.

"There's a malfunction here," Moriah told him. She lightly tapped the gauges, trying to get the needle to read properly. "I'll need to either switch machines or begin the reversal process."

"Give her a bolus of Versed to hold her, then go ahead and take her off the anesthesia machine," Blake suggested. "This is my last suture."

Moriah did as he'd recommended, then carefully monitored Marita after disconnecting her from the machine. "The gauge on the machine is broken, I think. We'll have to let the local doctors know."

"At least it lasted long enough to finish her surgery," was Blake's response. "She's all set."

"I'll take her over to the PACU, then." She quickly extubated the girl, then wheeled the gurney through the hall. In the PACU, Greta took a set of vital signs, then frowned.

"She's not breathing very well, Dr Howe."

Moriah frowned. "Is she waking up?"

Greta shook her head. "No."

Had she given the girl too much anesthesia? The machine could have been malfunctioning for minutes before she'd realized what had happened. Quickly, she came over and grabbed the ambu-bag. Placing the oxygen mask over Marita's face, she gave several breaths.

"Pulse ox better, up to 89 per cent," Greta informed her.

"Come on, Marita. Wake up," Moriah urged.

She gave several more breaths, then Marita began to thrash her head back and forth. Sighing in relief, Moriah removed the ambu-bag.

Marita's eyelids fluttered open, a sight Moriah had rarely been so thankful to see.

"Whew, that was close." Moriah turned toward Greta. "I'm going to put a note on the malfunctioning anesthesia machine, so this doesn't happen to someone else."

She stayed by Marita's bedside until the girl was fully recovered from her overdose of anesthesia. Finally, Moriah felt comfortable leaving. The rest of her evening was free.

And so was Blake's.

Moriah already knew exactly what she wanted to do. First, she'd check on Henri. Once she'd changed his hand dressing, she'd surprise Blake in his room. Not only had he given his all to his patients, he'd taken care of her more than once, with her injured ankle, then when she'd been ill. Heck, it was about time she did something for him.

A picnic? Maybe. She warmed to the idea, wondering what it would take to convince the hotel to make a couple of meals to go. Surely, once she and Blake were alone, they'd have plenty of time to talk. Or not to talk.

She'd wear something nice and slinky, just in case he wasn't clear on the message she wanted to send. No mixed signals allowed. Moriah grinned.

She couldn't wait to see the expression on his face.

Hours later, Moriah was finally ready. She held a large paper bag of food in one hand and smoothed down her sundress with the other. She hadn't brought anything sexy with her to Peru, but at least the dress was nice. And she wasn't wearing a stitch of underwear beneath.

Gathering her courage, she lifted a hand and knocked on Blake's door. When he didn't answer right away, she tapped her foot nervously.

Finally the door opened. Blake looked surprised to see her. "What is it? Something wrong?"

"Nothing's wrong. I brought a picnic for us." She lifted the bag and patted the blanket folded over her arm. "I hope you're hungry."

"Ah—actually, I've already eaten." Blake stood in the doorway, looking distinctly uncomfortable.

"That's all right, I'm not all that hungry for food myself," Moriah confessed. She leaned closer, standing on tiptoe to brush his jaw with a kiss. "A private party without food is just as good."

To her surprise, Blake grabbed her shoulders to prevent her from coming closer. "This isn't a good idea."

She frowned. "Why not? I thought we had an understanding, an agreement that this is a no-strings relationship."

"Really? Funny, I can't seem to recall that conversation." Blake's hands tightened momentarily, then relaxed. "Moriah, who are you trying to kid? I saw you with Rasha's baby and with Henri. You're not a no-strings type of woman."

She wasn't, and the truth was hard to deny. Still, she kept her tone light. "Would a relationship with me be so bad?"

"No. Yes. I mean—Damn." Blake dropped her shoulders and scrubbed his hands over his face. "I can't do this."

"What?"

"Keep lying to you. Or to myself."

A trickle of unease slithered down her spine. "Lying?"

"Lying to each other, as if this is going to work." His expression was pained. "I care about you, Moriah. For God's sake, I'm falling in love with you."

She felt her mouth drop open.

Had he really said he was falling in love with her? Tentative hope flared. "Really?"

"Yes, but you need to understand—I can't change who I am. I'm falling for you, but I still don't want a family."

Her brief feeling of euphoria faded. "You can't mean that."

"I do. You're the one who told me adults make choices. What if this is the choice I've made? Is it so awful just because it happens to be one you don't agree with?" When she opened her mouth to interrupt him, he raised a hand. "Do you see that as selfish? I think it's being realistic. Some people aren't the family type, they can't cope with it. My parents were a prime example."

His parents weren't worth much, in her opinion, but she held her tongue about that. "Children don't have to be a burden, Blake."

"Yet they are a burden, by their nature. They need to be loved, clothed, fed, housed and taken care of. Some people welcome that burden, others don't. Some people simply don't want families, Moriah. And I'm one of them." He stepped back, widening the distance between them. "If you can live with that part of me, then you're welcome to come in."

She stared at him, unable to believe he'd tossed her an ultimatum. He loved her and she loved him, but she couldn't accept what he was saying. No matter how badly she wanted him, she couldn't make herself step over the threshold. "Blake, I know you've lived most of your life alone. But I can't change who I am either. I come from a large family. I've always dreamed of having children." She shook her head. "I can't give up my dreams. Especially since I don't believe you're anything like your parents."

"You might not like it, but I am very much like my parents. I spent time with your family, Moriah. There were so many people, everyone talking at the same time with no one listening. I couldn't wait to leave. With every minute that passed, I knew I didn't belong there."

Her eyes widened. She'd had no idea he'd felt like that. And for the life of her she couldn't think of a suitable response.

"You have no idea how much I wish I could change for you. But I can't."

Slowly, quietly, giving her every chance to stop him, he closed the door.

Her knees threatened to buckle and she leaned against the wall for support. The bag of food slipped from her fingers to land on the floor with a thud.

She had so wanted to believe there was the slenderest hope of having a future with him.

But Blake had just convinced her there wasn't.

Moriah pulled herself together, knowing there wasn't a place in Peru she could go to avoid memories of Blake. She headed back to the hospital, where she could at least talk to her patients as a distraction.

Theo, Marita's father, was grateful for the dinner she brought him, the one she'd originally intended to give to Blake. The second meal she'd planned to give to Henri, since Marita wasn't able to eat anything except through a straw. Moriah had planned for that, though, stopping in the hospital cafeteria first to fetch a shake-like concoction made from papaya juice and milk.

"Have you seen how you look?" she asked Marita as the girl gratefully sipped her drink.

Slowly, Marita shook her head.

"I'll get the mirror for you." She hurried out to the nurses' station and fetched the mirror, then returned to Marita's room. "Here." She held up the mirror. "Take a look."

For a long moment Marita gazed at her reflection, then bright tears welled up in her eyes and rolled down her brown cheeks. Moriah muttered a curse and dropped the mirror on the bed. "Oh, Marita, don't cry. I know the incision looks a little puffy now, but it will heal beautifully, you'll see."

"It's OK, she's not upset." Theo stood and hugged his daughter with one arm. "She's crying tears of joy."

"She is?" Worried, Moriah tipped Marita's chin up with her fingers to look into the girl's eyes. "Really?"

Marita nodded. Her lip was swollen and sore, but she spoke slowly and quietly. "Thank you very much. You have given me a new life."

"You're welcome." Moriah wished all her patients could be this happy. She turned and headed down the hall to Henri's room carrying the second container of food.

"Hello, Henri. I brought dinner for you."

"Moriah." He was bouncing on the bed with the pent-up energy of youth. He looked happy to see her. "Thank you so much. Look what I can do." He raised his affected hand and moved all five of his fingers.

"Excellent." Moriah dropped into the chair beside him. "Now you'll need to keep up your exercises, so they become even more flexible."

"I will." He dug into the food with gusto. "And then maybe I get to leave tomorrow."

"So soon?" Moriah's stomach tensed. She'd really enjoyed spending this time with Henri. He was a great kid. And she couldn't help but wonder if this was the closest she'd get to having a family of her own. Taking care of Henri here, and playing with her nieces and nephews when she returned home.

Shaking herself out of her funk, she realized that if Henri was going home she'd need to arrange for transportation. Rather than head all the way back to the hotel, she went to the nurses' station to inquire about using their phone.

The Peruvian nurses seemed puzzled by her request, so she explained the whole story, how she needed to get Henri back to the orphanage once he was discharged. There was a bit of discussion about buses versus taxis, then one nurse generously offered Moriah the use of her car. Moriah didn't want to offend her by refusing, so she gratefully accepted, and they made arrangements to meet in front of the hotel the following morning.

Satisfied, Moriah returned to Henri's room. At least she could take Henri back where he belonged. And she imagined Sister Rita wouldn't let her get away a second time without the grand tour. Maybe she'd take the morning off.

After she'd checked Henri's hand incision, she settled in for the rest of the night.

There was no use going back to her hotel room—

she wouldn't get any more sleep there than she would sitting here by Henri's bed. She watched him sleep, his youthful expression peaceful. He was satisfied to have five fully movable fingers, and Marita was thankful for her new life.

She should be thrilled at the positive outcomes, yet she couldn't shake the cloak of depression that had settled over her shoulders. Blake thought he might be falling in love with her, but he only wanted her on his terms. She knew she loved him, but longed for a family.

What if she gave up Blake, only to discover she couldn't have children of her own? Or, worse, what if she never found a man she loved as much as she loved Blake to have a family with?

At first, she had seen Blake's refusal to have a family as being selfish.

But maybe she was really the selfish one. Because she wanted it all. Blake, marriage and a family.

And now she feared she'd end up with none of them.

The next morning, Moriah woke up with a stiff neck from the awkward position in which she'd slept in the chair beside Henri's bed. With a wry glance at the clock she knew Blake would be coming in soon. Pride, if nothing else, forced her into the bathroom to freshen up.

"Hi, Dr Powers." She heard Henri greet Blake and quickly finished in the bathroom.

"Hello, Blake." She gestured toward Henri. "I think your star patient is doing great."

"I can see that." Blake crossed the room and examined Henri's fingers. "He could probably be discharged, as long as he continues to take the full course of antibiotics."

"No problem. I'll make sure he knows how to take the medication before we leave."

"Have you arranged for Bernardo to drive you?" Blake asked.

"No, actually, I've made arrangements to borrow a car." Talking to him like this, like they were polite strangers rather than lovers, was difficult. She swallowed her instinctive offer to ask him to come along. "Don't worry, we'll be fine." She glanced at Henri. "Right?"

"Right," he echoed, but his gaze was troubled. Had Henri noticed the strain between her and Blake? He was a bright kid, she didn't doubt he'd pick up on the tension.

"Fine, then. Consider him discharged." Blake wrote the order on the chart, then handed her a discharge summary sheet, transcribed in Spanish on one side, English on the other. "This is for the staff at the orphanage."

"I know." She took the slip of paper, careful not to touch him in the process. For a long moment they stood awkwardly, then Blake turned to leave.

Moriah had to steel herself against the urge to call him back, even though she had no idea what she would say. Pushing aside her discontent, she gathered Henri's things together.

They walked down to the hospital lobby, so Moriah could fetch his antibiotics from the pharmacy. As they headed outside, she gave them to him, along with detailed instructions on how to take them. "Twice a day, one in the morning and one at night. Do you understand? Put them in your pocket so they won't get lost."

Henri complied, but remained quiet. Just outside the hospital entrance, she caught sight of Rasha and Manuel. Rasha saw her and waved wildly. She immediately crossed over to them.

"How's the baby?" She peered at the sleeping infant nestled in Manuel's muscular arms.

"Fine. Better now that she has the antibiotics."

"She's beautiful." Moriah squashed a surge of unattractive jealousy. Certainly, Rasha and Manuel deserved to be happy.

No use wondering why the same sort of happiness seemed to elude her.

"Please, you must come to the festival tomorrow night." Rasha exchanged a long look with her husband. "We would like to see you again before you return home."

"You couldn't keep me away," Moriah promised. "But for now we'd better get going, right, Henri?" She glanced down, but didn't see his familiar face anywhere. She frowned. "Hey, where did he go?"

Rasha and Manuel glanced at each other, then shook their heads. "I don't know," Manuel said.

The circular street was packed with people as the festival preparations were now in full swing.

"Maybe he went for a walk?" Rasha suggested.

For a walk? Where would he go? Back to the orphanage by himself? Not likely, without a ride. She dashed down the street, to the area in front of the hotel, but he wasn't there either. She quickly made her way back to the hospital, where Rasha and Manuel still waited.

Her shoulders slumped as she forced herself to face the truth. Henri was too responsible to simply wander off. He must have run away, to avoid returning to the orphanage.

CHAPTER TWELVE

BLAKE could barely concentrate. He must have relived the conversation with Moriah a thousand times, only now he changed the outcome. Instead of being bluntly honest and forcing her to decide between him and her dreams of having a family, he opened the door wider and pulled her inside, into his arms.

Damn. He should have stayed away from her. Because no matter what he'd said, he didn't really want her to change for him. The image of how she'd looked holding Rasha's baby daughter wouldn't leave him alone. He'd been bothered by a strange urge to hold the baby, too, when he'd never experienced anything remotely similar before.

Not every woman possessed the maternal instinct, but Moriah was a natural-born nurturer. Keeping a professional distance while talking to her a few minutes ago in Henri's room had almost killed him. She'd looked so stoic, so determined to ignore her feelings, he'd almost given in right then and there.

But then he'd remembered his childhood, and his parents. They hadn't wanted a baby, but he'd arrived on the scene anyway. He supposed they'd tried to adapt to his presence as much as they'd been able to, although his memories of those early years were blurred and faded.

The only clear image he could recall was of the day they'd taken him to the airport to put him on a plane bound for Chicago, where his aunt and uncle had lived. His parents had stood in the small airport, their arms wrapped around each other's waists, waving at him with wide smiles as the stewardess had taken him by the hand and led him aboard. To this day, he was left with the impression they had been a unit, so tightly paired even a child hadn't penetrated the bond.

It was a memory that still stuck with him, all these years later. Maybe Moriah was right: being abandoned by his parents had translated to avoiding close, intimate relationships. Until he'd made love with Moriah.

Now she was the only woman he could imagine having the sense of completeness with that his parents must have had. Yet she was the one woman who wouldn't settle for existing as half of a pair.

A no-win situation, no matter how you looked at it.

Outside José's room, he paused and braced his hand on the door frame, struggling to breathe around the tightness of his chest. Would he ever get over the feeling his insides were being ripped into shreds? Or would she haunt him for the rest of his life, ruining him for anyone else?

He was afraid he already knew the answer. Straightening, he took a deep breath and walked into José's room.

"Good morning. How are you feeling?"

"Fine. I'd like to go home soon. I need to return to work." José seemed to be a little more comfortable than the last time he'd checked on him.

"I understand." Blake took a few minutes to examine his patient, noticing the skin flap looked much better. Another success. He'd write the discharge orders as soon as he was finished making rounds.

He returned an hour later. Seated at the nurses' station, he'd just signed his name when Moriah rushed in, a determined glint in her eyes. "Blake, I need your help."

"What's wrong?" He quickly stood, raking his gaze over her.

"Henri ran away."

"What?" Blake was astounded by the news. "But why? I thought he'd adapted to life at the orphanage?"

"I thought so, too." Moriah ran an agitated hand through her hair. "All I know is that he's gone. One minute he was there, standing beside me while I talked to Rasha and Manuel, then, poof, he's gone. Vanished. I didn't know what to do so I came to find you."

"All right, we'll both go and look for him. He's only ten years old, he couldn't have gone far."

"I've checked the hotel, but that's all. Finding him will be hard because there are people everywhere, trying to finish the decorations for the festival."

Blake soon understood what she'd meant. Never had he seen the streets of Trujillo so crowded. There was hardly a car in sight, but everywhere he looked, people were setting up booths, lights and working on the stage for the festival.

"I'm sure he's not far. I'll help you look for him."

He recognized a few of the locals from the time he'd helped string up the lanterns and thought about requesting a search party, but figured he'd hold off for now. The boy probably hadn't gone far. He and Moriah would no doubt find Henri soon.

"It isn't like him, to take off like this."

"What was he wearing?" Blake asked her.

"White pants and a red short-sleeved T-shirt."

"All right, you go south, I'll head north. We'll meet here at the statue in twenty minutes."

Moriah nodded and took off. He headed in the opposite direction from the hotel, looking for anything that might have caught a child's eye. He quickened his pace when he noticed a whole group of kids gathered in front of what appeared to be a school.

"Henri?" It was hard to tell if a particular boy was there. Most of the children were dressed very much like Henri.

The crowd of kids parted and he saw what they had gathered around: a boy, lying on the ground. His heart jumped into his throat before he realized the supine child wasn't Henri. Then his expression cleared because Henri was there, using fabric from his pants leg to bind a bleeding cut on the boy's arm.

"What happened?" Blake pushed his way to the child's side.

"I saw them fighting and tried to stop it." Henri's right eye was puffy, as if he'd gotten in the way of someone's fist. "They didn't listen at first, not even when I shouted and shouted. Finally it was different when one of them was hurt. I tried to make a dressing for his arm, like the one you made for me in the hospital."

Relieved the crisis wasn't worse, he had to give the kid credit. Henri hadn't simply taken off, but had instead waded into the thick of things in an effort to help out. He laid a hand on Henri's shoulder, remembering how the boy had shared his dream of becoming a doctor. "You did a good job with the bandage," Blake complimented him. "Did he get hit in the head?"

Henri shook his head, but Blake did a quick assessment on the injured child anyway, to make sure there wasn't something really wrong with him.

"Open your eyes for me," he said in Spanish. To his relief, the boy's pupils were equal and reactive. As far as he could tell, there were no other injuries. He turned toward Henri. "Moriah is worried about you, Henri. We need to get this boy to the clinic and let Moriah know you're fine."

Henri nodded and between them they got the injured boy to his feet. Other than the cut on his arm, he seemed fine, but Blake intended to get him to the hospital to make sure.

He didn't see Moriah on the way as he took Henri and the injured boy to the clinic, where the locals took over his care. Blake stayed long enough to make sure he wasn't needed before he and Henri headed back to the statue in the center of the street, the designated meeting place.

Moriah rushed toward them, her expression a mixture of relief and anger. "Henri! I can't believe you ran away. Don't you ever do anything like that again, do you hear me?"

The boy shook his head. "I didn't run away. I—"

She continued as if he hadn't spoken. "You took off without saying a word. Do you have any idea how I felt when I noticed you were gone?"

Blake experienced a flash of sympathy for Henri, who couldn't manage to get a word in on his own behalf. He rested his hands protectively on the boy's shoulders. "Moriah, listen to him for a minute."

"Are you defending him?" Her tone sharpened.

Blake wanted to sigh. "All I'm saying is you need to give the kid a chance to tell his side of the story."

"All right." She drew a deep breath then crossed her arms over her chest. "What happened, Henri?"

"I saw the kids at the school." He glanced up at Blake as if seeking support. "I only moved a few feet away from you, so I could see them better. Then I realized one big kid was pushing a smaller kid."

"And that made you go closer?"

Henri nodded. "I only wanted to help. The bigger kids shouldn't hurt the littler ones."

"You wanted to help?" Moriah's expression betrayed a mixture of hope and disbelief. "You honestly didn't try to run away? You only wanted to stop the fight?"

He nodded. "At the orphanage, I help take care of the younger kids. They're not supposed to fight either. But they do." His exaggerated sigh was so adult-like, Blake had to bite back a smile.

Moriah knelt beside Henri, taking his arms in her hands and looking deep into his eyes. "Tell me the truth, Henri. Are you afraid to go back to the orphanage for some reason? Does anyone hurt you there?"

Henri shook his head emphatically. "No."

"All right, if you're sure." Moriah looked relieved. "Are you ready to go back now?"

He nodded. "Yes. I'm ready to go back." He ran his hand along the brightly colored ribbons woven into the wrought-iron fences. "But do you think Sister Rita will bring us back on the bus to see the festival? Because, if not, maybe I can stay lost for another day."

His expression was so earnest, so full of hope, Blake was tempted to help him out. Henri may have been born in Peru, but Blake felt a certain kinship with him just the same. He remembered, too well, how it felt to be the one left out of a party.

Maybe it wouldn't be the worst thing in the world, to give Henri a chance to experience one.

"No, absolutely not." Moriah couldn't believe Blake actually wanted to keep Henri for another day. "Blake, I promised Sister Rita I'd take him back after he was discharged. Then he scared me by wandering away. Why would I reward his irresponsible behavior?"

"Moriah, he didn't exactly wander away. The kids at the school caught his eye, he moved closer. You heard him, he only tried to help break up the fight."

Why Blake's sudden urge to stand up on Henri's behalf annoyed her so much was a complete mystery. Although she knew she was overreacting, her hands still shook from the surge of adrenaline she'd experienced when she'd discovered Henri gone. She twisted them together to hide them from view. "I don't think it's a good idea," she repeated stubbornly.

"All right, we'll take him back and try to convince

Sister Rita to bring all the kids to the festival." Blake had the audacity to exchange a knowing wink with Henri.

"We?" She raised a brow. "I'm the one who arranged the ride, I'll take him back. And you shouldn't make rash promises you may not be able to keep."

"You're in no condition to drive, Moriah." His voice was soft, but she couldn't mistake the edge of determination underlying his tone. "So if you're set on taking him back, we'll take him together."

He was right, although it galled her to admit it. "Fine. We'll take him back together."

"Good. Now, just give me a few minutes to change my clothes." When she opened her mouth to protest, he gestured to the juice cart across the street. "Get something cold for yourself. Henri, why don't you come with me? I'll only be gone a few minutes."

Henri eagerly went along with Blake. With a sigh she realized she didn't have much choice but to wait as Blake and Henri disappeared into the hotel.

She bought the three of them a soft drink, then found a place to sit by the statue to drink hers.

The festival preparations continued and she stared at the brightly colored skirts and gauzy tops which she would have been tempted to buy if she hadn't been so upset.

Sister Rita had placed Henri in her care. She'd only taken her eyes off him for a few minutes, to talk to Rasha and Manuel, when he had suddenly disappeared.

Guilt flooded her. If Henri had been younger, or if

something bad had happened to him, she'd never have forgiven herself.

Was this heavy responsibility partly why Blake had decided against having a family himself?

Moriah glanced up when Henri and Blake approached. They were engaged in a serious discussion. Blake was very attractive with his golden hair and tanned skin, emphasized by his white T-shirt and casual tan pants. She was surprised when he and Henri stopped to chat with a couple of the local men for a few minutes, before continuing toward her.

"Are you ready to go?" Blake asked.

She wanted to ask what they had been talking about, but decided they'd asked about the festival. Especially since Blake seemed hell-bent on having the kids from the orphanage attend. "Yes. Here's your juice." Moriah handed the soft drinks to them, then gestured to the hotel. "I hope our ride is still available."

Luckily, the car promised by the Peruvian nurse was still waiting for them in front of the hotel. Gratefully, she took the keys from Freda's patient hands.

"Thank you so much, Freda. I'll return the car to you very soon." Moriah gestured at Henri. "Go on, get in."

"Do you have any clue how to get there?" Blake asked.

She only had a vague idea, but nodded anyway. "Pretty much. I asked the hotel manager last night for directions." She'd been too preoccupied with kissing Blake to remember the route Bernardo had taken on the way out to pick Henri up.

"All right. I'll drive, you navigate." Blake plucked the keys from her fingers and slid into the driver's seat.

She supposed it didn't matter which of them sat behind the wheel, but she had wanted to experience the thrill of driving in Peru for herself. Graciously, she took the passenger seat.

The trip didn't take long at all since there wasn't much traffic on the road leading to the orphanage. They passed a few buses, though, one seemingly filled with kids. Henri chatted about the bus ride he'd taken on his last trip to town. According to his version of the story, a swerving taxi had almost crashed into them. He hadn't been afraid, though. To him, the whole experience had been an adventure.

Sister Rita was waiting for them at the front door. She didn't dress like a conventional nun, but wore the brightly colored skirts and gauzy blouses the local women favored. Moriah held onto Henri's shoulder, half expecting him to bolt, but he readily climbed the stairs and greeted the sister with a smile.

"*Hola*, Sister. Where's Bonita?" he asked.

"Inside, waiting for you." Sister Rita stepped back, gesturing for the adults to follow. "Come in, please. Have some juice. I would like to thank you for bringing Henri back and for fixing his hand."

Obviously the woman hadn't noticed Henri's black eye, or she would have known better than to thank her. Still, Moriah wasn't about to enlighten Sister Rita by telling her how close they'd come to not bringing him back. And she couldn't shake the suspicion he'd been trying to avoid the orphanage. She forced a smile. "You're welcome."

The orphanage was a sprawling stucco ranch-style

building, surprisingly cool considering the heat of the desert. Sister Rita led them through a narrow hallway to a spacious kitchen seemingly overflowing with fruit and bread. Henri was already inside and Moriah was surprised to find him hugging a young girl, lifting her off her feet.

"Henri," the girl squealed. "You're back! You're back!"

"*Sí*, Bonita, I'm back." After setting her back down, he turned to face them. "Bonita, I'd like you to meet Señor Blake and Señorita Moriah. They are the North American doctors who fixed my hand so I can learn a proper craft." His smile was so bright, Moriah was nearly blinded by his pride. "This is my little sister, Bonita."

His sister? Stunned, Moriah could only stare at the two of them. She'd had no idea Henri had a younger sister. But seeing them together now, the family resemblance was remarkable. They had the same lively, dancing eyes, high cheekbones and identical smiles. No sibling rivalry in evidence here, not when she saw the way Henri kept a protective arm around Bonita's shoulders.

Her suspicion dissolved in a puddle of shame. Good grief. There was no way Henri had ever intended to run away from the orphanage. She could tell by his actions that he'd never leave his little sister behind.

And she knew why. Because siblings stuck together, no matter what.

CHAPTER THIRTEEN

BLAKE glanced at Moriah for the tenth time in as many minutes. She wasn't sleeping, but staring pensively out of the car window.

"Are you all right?" he asked finally.

"I guess." Her listless tone suggested otherwise. "It's been a long day."

"Yeah." He wondered what was going on in that busy mind of hers. They'd stayed longer than they'd planned at the orphanage. Moriah's gaze had been constantly drawn to Bonita, Henri's younger sister, as if she was enthralled with the girl. He had to admit, she was a cutie.

He'd felt a strange, tightening sensation in the center of his chest when he'd seen Moriah seated on the floor between Henri and Bonita, laughing at the pictures they'd drawn. In that brief moment he'd seen Moriah's future. With her dark hair and native American heritage, the two children could have easily been hers.

Adoption was an interesting concept. Hadn't he been pretty much adopted by his aunt and uncle? What would have happened if he'd been sent to live with an aunt and uncle and their six kids? If he'd grown up with a household of cousins, would he have always felt like an outsider, as he had with Moriah's rambunctious family? Or would he have grown into the concept of being one of the gang?

Not that he could change how he had been raised. It was too late for him to adjust now.

Wasn't it?

He'd ended up spending some time with the kids alone, while Moriah had gone off to have a private conversation with Sister Rita. He'd had a strange sense of pride when Henri had showed him how he was progressing in his studies. And Bonita's artwork had been truly amazing.

He'd never considered it before now, but kids were really the essence of hope. What would his future hold without them?

Was this hope exactly what Moriah saw when she thought about having a family?

When it had been time to leave the orphanage, Moriah had been reluctant to let Henri go. Moriah's gaze was pensive, yet she didn't talk about what she and Sister Rita had discussed.

All this time, he'd thought Moriah's family were close because of some inherent tendency, a bond arising from the genes that had been passed down to her and her brothers and sisters from her parents.

But he got the distinct impression that Moriah felt just as close to Henri and Bonita, even without the bond of blood.

"Do you think Sister Rita will bring the children to the festival tomorrow?" Moriah asked.

"I think so." Blake had liked the director of the orphanage immediately. She didn't take any grief from the children, but ruled with grace and compassion. "I have a feeling it was the plan all along."

"Good. I'd love to see Bonita and Henri again." Her voice was full of longing.

Actually, he was surprised to admit he felt the same way. He didn't quite understand why. He fell silent, aware their own time together in Peru was almost at an end. Just a couple of days and they'd be on a plane back to the United States.

Last year they'd spent their last evening in Peru together, dining and laughing with silliness, until George had found them to give them the message about Ryan's death.

But then he'd hurt Moriah, just like Ryan had. And he could even admit he'd hurt himself by being with the wrong woman. His fingers tightened on the steering wheel of their borrowed car. He wished more than anything she'd been willing to take him the way he was, because he wanted nothing more than to whisk Moriah away to the privacy of his hotel room, where he could make sweet love to her all night long.

"You just passed the hotel," Moriah observed.

"Damn." He quickly circled the statue and headed back to the hotel. "Sorry about that."

"No problem." She hesitated. "I told Freda we'd leave the car here. She plans to pick it up after her shift at the hospital later tonight."

"Sounds good. I'll leave the key with the hotel manager."

"Well." She cleared her throat. "Thanks for coming along with me. We're not operating tomorrow, so maybe I'll see you at the festival."

Tomorrow seemed like a lifetime away, but he knew she was right. Besides, he had to head back to the hospital to see if George needed any help. He'd been gone long enough as it was.

"I'd like that," he agreed.

"Great. See you later, then." She ducked out of the car, and headed inside. He watched her as she greeted the hotel manager as warmly as if he were a long-lost friend, and a stunning realization hit him broadside.

He loved her. Had, in fact, loved her for years. And all the traits he loved about her were the same ones that would make her a perfect wife and mother.

He couldn't bear the thought of Moriah becoming the heart and soul of some other man's family.

Moriah couldn't believe how the city had been transformed. Crowds of people laughed and shouted as they swarmed in the street. The brightly painted stucco houses were all decorated, either with flags or the bright ribbons woven through the wrought-iron fences. A spicy scent of fish intermingled with the tart papaya juice and the yeasty Peruvian beer added to the party atmosphere. The Trujillo Festival was in full swing.

Moriah eyed the beer, wondering if she'd dare to try some herself later on.

Children played games while doting parents watched.

She'd gotten to the festival later than she'd planned and searched the crowds for Henri and Bonita.

She was surprised to find them with Blake. The three of them were in the middle of the children's games, throwing balls in an effort to knock over three stacked bottles. There weren't prizes to win, but with Blake's encouragement the kids played with enthusiasm anyway. She shook her head in amazement—some games knew no boundaries.

When Henri saw her, he took Bonita's hand and crossed over to meet her. "*Hola*, Moriah. We've been looking for you."

"And now you found me." She gave them each a quick hug. Then her eyes met Blake's, an unspoken question in her eyes. "I had to work late, or I would have been here sooner. Seems like you had fun with Blake, though."

"Can we stay late enough to see the band play?" Henri wanted to know.

"Probably not. Didn't Sister Rita say her bus was leaving soon?" Blake reminded them.

Moriah nodded. "Yes, and you can see the band hasn't quite started yet. Maybe you'll have time to hear one song, but that might be all." In fact, the stage was already set up, the musicians gathering and tuning their instruments. Apparently with the band came dancing.

"Aw, we wanted to watch the dancing."

Moriah led them over to the closest street vendor. "Are you guys hungry? Thirsty?"

"Thirsty," Bonita declared firmly.

Before she could do anything, Blake fetched juice

for all of them. The four of them had just sat down to enjoy the treat when she noticed Sister Rita making her way toward her.

"I told the children to return to the bus at seven o'clock." Her brows were pulled together in a mock frown. "But I can see they were too distracted to listen."

"My fault, I guess," Moriah apologized, glancing at her watch in dismay. "I didn't get here until late, I was hoping to spend more time with them."

"Henri, Bonita, you must return to the bus, all right?" Sister Rita directed.

"Goodbye, Blake. Goodbye, Moriah. Thanks for the juice." Henri and Bonita gave her and Blake quick hugs.

Moriah could hardly stand to let them go. "You're more than welcome. Now, don't forget to write to me, all right? I'll be looking forward to your letters."

Both kids nodded earnestly. "We will."

"Go on now, run along." Sister Rita shooed them off. "I need to talk to Moriah for a moment."

"Well, if you want to talk, I'll just go along with the kids." Blake graciously left the two women alone.

What had possessed Blake to spend the day with the kids? A change of heart? She was afraid to hope. Moriah waved until the kids were out of sight.

"I've been thinking about your question, Moriah," Sister Rita said slowly. "I told you Americans were not normally allowed to adopt Peruvian children very easily."

Moriah nodded. "Yes, I remember." She'd been

sorely disappointed with the news. Naively, she'd assumed orphan children from Peru would be easy for anyone to adopt.

"While it's not easy, there are ways to appeal to our government. I would be willing to help, if you like."

Her eyes widened. "Really?"

"Yes." Sister Rita nodded and handed her a packet of papers. "Here is some information about our adoption process, light reading for your trip home. I'm hoping once you review all the requirements, you won't be put off by the amount of time, energy and effort it will take for you to adopt Henri and Bonita."

"Don't worry, I won't." Moriah grinned and tucked the packet of papers under her arm. "Thank you, Sister. I'll be in touch, I promise."

"I believe you will." Sister Rita took Moriah's hand in hers and clasped it warmly. "Yes, I do believe you will. Things will work out, if God means for them to be."

Moriah wished she could truly believe the sentiment, especially with regard to Blake, but she held her tongue and watched the nun hustle away, herding the rest of the orphanage children toward the bus. Blake seemed to have disappeared, so she turned away.

She headed toward the hotel, intent on putting the adoption paperwork in a safe place. Moriah figured she should be thrilled with the news that adopting Henri and Bonita was a possibility. The decision felt right. She could picture them with her family so easily.

But there was still a gaping hole in her heart, because her family would never be complete without Blake.

She loved him. She'd fallen in love with him a year ago right here in sunny Peru. This was their last night together.

Tomorrow they would drive to Lima, get on a plane and fly home. Her time with Blake was almost over, this time for good. Unless she gave up the idea of having a family, and accepted Blake on his terms.

Indecision gnawed at her. She couldn't imagine making such a sacrifice.

"Moriah?" Blake was glad he'd found her, having lost track of her after he'd ushered the kids to the bus. He'd been startled to find Moriah wearing the colorful skirt and nearly sheer gauzy blouse of the locals. She was dazzling, her hair softly waving about her shoulders, her white blouse emphasizing the olive tone of her skin. He crossed over to her, as if drawn by an invisible string.

"Hi, Blake." Moriah smiled at him, then gestured toward the stage where the Marinera folk band began playing a sultry tempo, encouraging the festival crowd to dance. "There's Rasha and Manuel, dancing on the stage. I bet Rasha's mother is babysitting for them. Aren't they wonderful?"

Blake immediately saw what had caught her attention. The women were wearing gauze blouses and bright skirts with gold bracelets lining their arms, and as they danced they enticed their male partners to join them. He recognized Rasha and Manuel in the center of the group.

Their hips moved in sexy rotations, promising unspoken pleasure. The two of them looked as if they were alone on the stage, unaware of anyone but each other. As much as they'd started a family with their new baby daughter, they were obviously a couple in love first and foremost. Blake felt the erotic beat of the music in his own pulse thundering in his ears.

"Rasha is so beautiful. I can't believe she's out there, just a couple of weeks after having a baby."

Blake dragged his gaze back to her. "I think you're beautiful, Moriah. Although tonight you look more Peruvian than American."

Self-consciously, she lifted a portion of her skirt. "I couldn't resist. The dress seems fitting for the evening."

"Dance with me?" He grasped her hand and pulled her closer.

She hesitated, then willingly flowed into his arms. He buried his face in the lemony scent of her hair, moving slowly and enjoying the sultry beat even as he wished like hell they were someplace alone.

"Mmm. I didn't realize you were such an incredible dancer," Moriah whispered.

He wanted to share far more with her than simply dancing, but right now he was more than content to hold her in his arms, to feel the light swish of her skirt against his legs, the firm pressure of her breasts pressed against his chest. His heart swelled with longing.

How on earth could he manage to let her go?

Very simply, he couldn't.

She pressed her mouth to the pulse in his neck and his thoughts fried in a spark of passion. He wanted her here and now, regardless of all the reasons he shouldn't.

Holding her tight, he angled his head until he could cover her mouth with his, teasing her lips apart and exploring deep.

They could have been the only two people on the entire dance floor for all he cared. He took his time, kissing her thoroughly, until she weakly clung to him, pressing urgently against him, silently asking for more.

He tore his mouth from hers, gasping for breath. "Moriah, please, let me take you back to my room."

"Yes." Her simple answer only fueled a new spurt of desire.

Easing away, he scanned the crowd, seeking the path of least resistance, the shortest distance to their hotel. Determined, he set forth, pitying any poor person who managed to get in their way as he navigated through the crush of the crowd.

"A bus accident!" someone shouted in Spanish. A few more local voices chimed in. "A bus crashed into a rock off the road. Just a few miles from here!"

"What did they say?" Moriah stopped cold, grasping his arm in a tight grip. "A bus accident?"

"Yes." For a nanosecond, he deeply resented the intrusion on these last few hours he had with Moriah, but he knew just as quickly that they needed to go to help. "We'd better see what we can do to help."

"Oh, my God, Blake. I hope it's not the bus carrying the kids back to the orphanage." Her eyes grew as wide as saucers. "Henri and Bonita are on that bus."

CHAPTER FOURTEEN

HENRI and Bonita? For a moment, he couldn't think, couldn't breathe. Accidents were far more horrible when children were involved. He could easily imagine the twisted metal blocking them in. The thought of those two kids being hurt, or worse, drove him forward. "Let's go."

A good portion of the crowd surged in the same direction, so he held fast to Moriah's hand and quickened his pace. The roads were blocked off for the festival, so there was no way to hail a taxi to take them to the scene.

Moriah was wearing a pair of sexy strappy sandals. She stopped briefly, just long enough to pull them off and carry them, so she could keep up.

Ahead, at a fork in the road, he saw the bus lying on its side. His gut twisted and a red haze blurred his vision when he heard crying and shouting from the injured people inside. He couldn't tell if they were adults or children, so he began to run.

Not Henri or Bonita. Don't let anyone be badly hurt, especially not Henri or Bonita.

"It's blue—just like the orphanage bus," Moriah gasped between panting breaths.

Lots of the buses here were blue, so he tried not to think the worst. He reached the bus along with several locals. The doorway was blocked, so a couple of men had already climbed the side of the bus to go in through a window.

He did the same thing, making his way to the first open window he could find. It was a tight squeeze, but finally he was in.

A quick glance confirmed there were some adults but mostly children on board.

"Shh, it's OK, tell me where it hurts." He stopped at the first crying child to examine the bleeding cut on the boy's arm, determining it would need stitches. The bruise on his forehead meant a possible head injury, too, but not too bad considering the boy was conscious enough to cry.

"Over here, Blake." Moriah poked her head through the window he'd crawled through. "We need to start getting these kids out."

She had a good point. "All right, here you go." The child was small enough so he could lift him through the window, enough for Moriah to get him the rest of the way out.

He moved on to the next child, subconsciously seeking the familiar faces of Henri and Bonita as he cared for the next injury. Over and over again, he lifted injured children out of the bus.

Soon only the adults were left and they weren't hurt too badly either, although getting them up through the windows was a more difficult task.

When they had the bus emptied of victims, Blake crawled up through the window into the night. He glanced at Moriah, who gave him a tired smile.

"This is a bus from Chimbote, not the orphanage," she told him quickly. "No fatalities and mostly minor injuries. Quite a few have been taken to the hospital for treatment."

His shoulders slumped in relief although he suspected his rapidly beating heart would take a little longer to return to normal. "Thank God. I'm glad it wasn't worse."

"Me, too." Moriah tilted her head curiously. "I don't think I've ever seen you so upset."

With a frown he took her arm and began to walk back toward the now sparsely populated festival. "Of course I'm upset at the thought of a potential busload of seriously injured kids. Who wouldn't be?"

"Do you think we should head over to the hospital, just to make sure they have enough staff on hand to handle the workload?" Moriah asked.

"Not a bad idea," Blake acknowledged.

There wasn't a lot of time to talk. But his fear and worry over the kids stayed with him. All too soon they were at the hospital, helping to provide aid as needed to the series of cuts, bruises and broken bones.

But much later, when he returned to his hotel room, he forced himself to admit the truth.

Entering the bus had been difficult, as he'd steeled himself against the possibility of finding an injured Henri or Bonita. He'd always considered kids to be a fair amount of responsibility. But somehow the two kids had wormed their way into his heart, without him even being aware of it.

Spending the day at the festival with Henri and Bonita had shown him they each had their own distinct personalities. They were already adults in the making. And his caring about them wasn't exactly a choice, but a fact. Pretty much like falling in love with Moriah.

Emotions weren't ruled by logic. Adults had choices to a certain point, but then emotion took over. He finally understood. Love, the most intense emotion of all, was the main reason parents chose to take on this very overwhelming responsibility of raising kids.

Moriah headed back to her room, having lost Blake in the confusion at the hospital. Luckily, the injuries sustained by those in the bus accident weren't serious, but just the volume alone had been more than the single ED doctor and two nurses had been able to handle.

When she walked outside, though, to get back to her hotel room, she'd been sad to see the festival was over.

She and Blake had only had time for one dance, although it had been one heck of a dance. Opening the door to her room, she sighed, realizing she missed him already.

Closing the door behind her, she forced herself not to dwell on her sorrow. She needed to pack her clothes. The bus was picking them up at six o'clock sharp for the long ride back to the airport in Lima.

coaching along the way. Kids don't come with instruction manuals, do they?"

She laughed. "No."

His tone turned serious. "I've realized something, Moriah. Love is caring about someone and accepting all aspects of them, the good and the bad and everything in between. Including things you might not understand at first."

She wanted to believe him, she really did. "I don't want to force you into this, Blake, and I don't want you to make a mistake. Maybe…maybe we should hold off on this whole adoption thing until you're sure?"

He stilled. "You'd do that for me?"

"I— Yes, I would." Now that she'd said the words, she knew she actually believed them. "I love you, too, Blake. And I've also loved you for years. And that means I love all of you, even the part of you that doesn't want children."

"You mean, the part of me that used not to want children," he corrected softly. "I figure it will take a while to get through this adoption process. Maybe we can talk it through while we wait…but I was going to suggest…' He swallowed. 'If you thought it would help to speed things up, we could get married right away."

Moriah slowly rose to her feet, stunned by his offer. "You need to be sure about this, Blake. Remember what you're getting into. For one thing, the adoption isn't guaranteed. The Peruvian government might turn us down. And for another—you told me once how my family made you feel claustrophobic. You couldn't wait to leave."

Blake grimaced. "I'll be honest, your family is a group that will take some getting used to. Would you mind starting slow? Maybe this time you could introduce me to just one or two siblings at a time, instead of the whole bunch?"

She laughed. "No, I don't mind starting slow. I guess my family can be overpowering."

His expression grew determined. "I want to make you happy, Moriah."

"And I want the same thing for you, too." She stepped closer. "Nothing is as important as you, Blake. Something I shouldn't have lost sight of. Marriage is a huge commitment in and of itself. A couple remains married long after their kids are grown and gone."

Blake slowly nodded. "Either way, I'm willing to work at this, Moriah, for the rest of my life. Are you?"

Stunned, she nodded. She simply couldn't think of anything to say, but thankfully he reached out to pull her into his arms and covered her mouth with his so that she didn't need to answer him at all.

She was more than willing to lose herself in his kiss, but he drew back, looking down at her with a question in his eyes.

"So was that your answer?"

Dazed, she stared at him. "You might need to repeat the question."

He grinned and reached out to tuck a lock of hair behind her ear. The brush of his fingertips against her skin made her shiver. "Will you marry me? Will you have a family with me?"

"Yes, I'll marry you." She kissed him again, tugging him toward the bed. "And I'll consider having a family with you. But we might need to practice for a while first."

"A woman after my own heart." Blake chuckled as he followed her down onto the bed, and the carefree tone of his laughter had never sounded so sweet.